Purity Plus Clarity Equals Power . . .

"Cassandra," he said.

Cassie's knees felt weak.

It was a voice of a shadow. A dark, liquid voice. So quiet, so insidious—so *evil*. Under his hematite-black eyes, she felt naked, exposed. As if he were looking into her mind. Looking for a crack to get in.

"Mr. Brunswick," she said. Her voice sounded strange to her own ears. Polite, but distant.

"So brave," he said. "I'm proud of you."

He turned away from Cassie. The fire leaped and crackled and Cassie felt her pulse in her throat and fingertips. *I can't stand much more of this,* she thought.

He began to turn around. He was facing her.

She saw the elegant black jacket, the black turtleneck sweater. But above the turtleneck was a monstrosity that forced tears from her eyes and clogged the scream in her throat. The man had no face.

No hair, no eyebrows, no eyes, no nose. No mouth, only a grinning outline of clenched teeth. Even that, even the stark bones that faced her, were as clear as water.

"You see, Cassandra," came the inhuman voice from behind those clenched teeth, "I have more power than you children have ever dreamed of."

BOOKS BY L. J. SMITH

THE VAMPIRE DIARIES

THE SECRET CIRCLE TRILOGY

The Night of the Solstice

Heart of Valor

Published by HarperPrism

ATTENTION: ORGANIZATIONS AND CORPORATIONS
Most HarperPaperbacks are available at special quantity discounts for bulk purchases for sales promotions, premiums, or fund-raising. For information please call or write:
**Special Markets Department, HarperCollins Publishers Inc., 10 East 53rd Street, New York, NY 10022–5299.
Telephone: (212) 207–7528. Fax: (212) 207–7222.**

The Secret Circle

Volume III

The Power

L. J. Smith

HarperPrism

A Division of HarperCollinsPublishers

HarperPrism
A Division of HarperCollins*Publishers*
10 East 53rd Street, New York, NY 10022–5299

A mass market edition of this book was published in 1992
by HarperPaperbacks.

A special edition was printed in 1995.

Produced by Daniel Weiss Associates, Inc.,
33 West 17th Street, New York, NY 10011.

First HarperPrism printing: November 1999

Printed in the United States of America

ISBN 0–06–106719–9

HarperCollins®, 📖®, and HarperPrism® are trademarks of
HarperCollins Publishers Inc.

Visit HarperPrism on the World Wide Web at
http://www.harpercollins.com

❖ 10 9 8 7 6

For Lauren and Brian,
who know love is the Power

The Power

ONE

"Diana, I have a little surprise for you," Faye said.

Diana's emerald eyes, with their thick sooty lashes, were swimming already. She still hadn't recovered from the shocks of tonight, and her face was strained as she stared at Faye.

Well, there was worse to come.

Now that it was finally going to happen, Cassie felt a curious sense of freedom. No more hiding, no more lying and evading. The nightmare was here at last.

"I suppose I should have told you before, but I didn't want to *upset* you," Faye was saying. Her eyes burned golden with a savage inner fire.

Adam, who wasn't stupid, glanced from Cassie to Faye and obviously came to a quick, if shattering, conclusion. He swiftly cupped a hand under Diana's elbow.

"Whatever it is can wait," he said. "Cassie ought to go and see her mother, and—"

"No, it can't *wait*, Adam Conant," Faye interrupted. "It's time Diana found out what sort of people she has around her." Faye whirled to face Diana again, her pale skin glowing with strange elation against the midnight-dark mane of her hair. "The ones you've *chosen*," she said to her cousin. "Your dearest friend—and *him*. The incorruptible Sir Adam. Do you want to know the reason you couldn't make it as leader? Do you want to know how naive you really are?"

Everyone was gathering close now, staring. Cassie could see varying degrees of bewilderment and suspicion in their expressions. The full moon shining from the west was so bright that it cast shadows, and it illuminated every detail of the scene.

Cassie looked at each of them: tough Deborah, beautiful Suzan with her perfect face marred by a puzzled frown, cool Melanie, and graceful, elfin Laurel. She looked at Chris and

Doug Henderson, the wild twins, who were standing by the slinking figure of Sean, and at icily handsome Nick behind them.

Finally she looked at Adam.

He was still holding Diana's arm, but his proud, arresting face was tense and alert. His eyes met Cassie's and something like understanding flashed between them, and then Cassie looked away, ashamed. She had no right to lean on Adam's strength. She was about to be exposed for what she was in front of the entire Circle.

"I kept hoping they would do the decent thing and control themselves," Faye said. "For their own sake, if not yours. But, obviously—"

"Faye, what are you *talking* about?" Diana interrupted, her patience splintering.

"Why, about Cassie and Adam, of course," Faye said, slowly opening her golden eyes wide. "About how they've been fooling around behind your back."

The words fell like stones into a tranquil pool. There was a long moment of utter silence, then Doug Henderson threw back his head and laughed.

"Yeah, an' my mom's a topless dancer," he jeered.

"And Mother Teresa's really Catwoman," said Chris.

"Come on, Faye," Laurel said sharply. "Don't be ridiculous."

Faye smiled.

"I don't blame you for not believing me," she said. "I was shocked too. But you see, it all started before Cassie came to New Salem. It started when she met Adam down on Cape Cod."

The silence this time had a different quality. Cassie saw Laurel look quickly at Melanie. Everyone knew that Cassie had spent several weeks on the Cape last summer. And everyone knew that Adam had been down in that area too, looking for the Master Tools. Cassie saw the dawning of startled understanding on the faces around her.

"It all started on the beach there," Faye went on. She was obviously enjoying herself, as she always enjoyed being the center of attention. She looked sexy and commanding as she wet her lips and spoke throatily, addressing the entire group although her words were meant for Diana. "It was love at first sight, I guess— or at least they couldn't keep their hands off each other. When Cassie came up here she even wrote a poem about it. Now how did that go?" Faye tilted her head to one side and recited:

"Each night I lie and dream about the one
Who kissed me and awakened my desire
I spent a single hour with him alone
And since that hour, my days are laced
with fire."

"That's right; that was her poem," Suzan said. "*I* remember. We had her in the old science building and she didn't want us to read it."

Deborah was nodding, her petite face twisted in a scowl. "I remember too."

"You may also remember how strange they both acted at Cassie's initiation," Faye said. "And how Raj seemed to *take* to Cassie so quickly, always jumping up on her and licking her and all. Well, it's very simple really—it's because they'd known each other before. They didn't want any of *us* to know that, of course. They tried to hide it. But eventually they got caught. It was the night we first used the crystal skull in Diana's garage—Adam was taking Cassie home, I guess. I wonder how *that* got arranged."

Now it was the turn of Laurel and Melanie to

look startled. Clearly they remembered the night of the first skull ceremony, when Diana had asked Adam to walk Cassie home, and Adam, after a brief hesitation, had agreed.

"They thought they were alone on the bluff—but somebody was watching. Two little somebodies, two little friends of mine . . ." Lazily, Faye worked her fingers, with their long, scarlet-tipped nails, as if stroking something. A flash of comprehension lighted Cassie's mind.

The *kittens*. The damned little bloodsucking kittens that lived wild in Faye's bedroom. Faye was saying the *kittens* were her spies? That she could communicate with them?

Cassie felt a chill at her core as she looked at the tall, darkly beautiful girl, sensing something alien and deadly behind those hooded golden eyes. She'd wondered all along who Faye had meant when she talked about her "friends" who saw things and reported back to her, but she'd never imagined this. Faye smiled in feline satisfaction and nodded at her.

"I have lots of secrets," she said directly to Cassie. "That's only one of them. But anyway," she said to the rest of the group, "it was that night they got caught. They were—

well, kissing. That's the polite way to put it. The kind of kissing that starts spontaneous combustion. I suppose they just couldn't resist their lustful passions any longer." She sighed.

Diana was looking at Adam now, looking for a denial. But Adam, his jaw set, was staring straight ahead at Faye.

Diana's lips parted with the quick intake of her breath.

"And it wasn't the only time, I'm afraid," Faye continued, examining her nails with an expression of demure regret. "They've been doing it ever since, stealing secret moments when you weren't looking, Diana. Like at the Homecoming dance—what a *pity* you weren't there. They started kissing right in the middle of the dance floor. I guess maybe they went somewhere more private afterward . . ."

"That's not true," Cassie cried, realizing even as she said it that she was virtually confirming that everything else Faye had said *was* true.

Everyone was looking at Cassie now, and there was no more jeering from the Hendersons. Their tilted blue-green eyes were focused and intent.

"I *wanted* to tell you," Faye said to Diana, "but Cassie just begged me not to. She was hysterical, crying and pleading—she said she would just *die* if you found out. She said she'd do anything. And that," Faye sighed, looking off into the distance, "was when she offered to get me the skull."

"*What?*" said Nick, his normally imper-. turbable face reflecting disbelief.

"Yes." Faye's eyes dropped to her nails again, but she couldn't keep a smile from curling the corners of her lips. "She knew I wanted to examine the skull, and she said she'd get it for me if I didn't tell. Well, what could I do? She was like a crazy person. I just didn't have the *heart* to refuse her."

Cassie sank her teeth into her lower lip. She wanted to scream, to protest that it hadn't been that way . . . but what was the use?

Melanie was speaking. "And I suppose you didn't have the heart to refuse the skull, either," she said to Faye, her gray eyes scornful.

"Well . . ." Faye smiled deprecatingly. "Let's put it this way—it was just too good a chance to miss."

"This isn't funny," Laurel cried. She looked stricken. "I still don't believe it—"

"Then how do you think she knew where to dig up the skull tonight?" Faye said smoothly.

"She stayed over at your house, Diana, the night we traced the dark energy to the cemetery. And she snuck around and figured out where the skull was buried by reading your Book of Shadows—but only after she stole the key to the walnut cabinet and checked there." Gleeful triumph shone out of Faye's golden eyes; she couldn't conceal it any longer.

And nobody in the group could deny the truth of Faye's words any longer. Cassie *had* known where to dig up the skull. There was no way to get around that. Cassie could see it happening in face after face: the ending of disbelief and the slow beginning of grim accusation.

It's like *The Scarlet Letter*, Cassie thought wildly as she stood apart with all of them looking at her. She might as well be standing up on a platform with an A pinned to her chest. Helplessly, she straightened her back and tried to hold her chin level, forcing herself to look back at the group. I will not cry, she thought. I will not look away.

Then she saw Diana's face.

Diana's expression was beyond stricken. She seemed simply paralyzed, her green eyes wide and blank and shattered.

"She swore to be loyal and faithful to the Circle, and never to harm anyone inside it," Faye was saying huskily. "But she lied. I suppose it's not surprising, considering she's half outsider. Still, I think it's gone on long enough; she and Adam have had enough time to enjoy themselves. So now you know the truth. And now," Faye finished, looking over the ravaged members of the Circle, and especially her deathly still cousin, with an air of thoughtful gratification, "we'd probably better be getting home. It's been a long night." Lazily, smiling faintly, she started to move away.

"No." It was a single word, but it stopped Faye in her tracks and it made everyone else turn toward Adam.

Cassie had never seen his blue-gray eyes look this way before—they were like silver lightning. He moved forward with his usual easy stride. There was no violence in the way he caught Faye's arm, but the grip must have been like iron—Cassie could tell that because Faye couldn't get away from it. Faye looked down at his fingers in offended surprise.

"You've had your turn," Adam said to her. His voice was carefully quiet, but the words dropped from his lips like chips of white-hot steel. "Now it's mine. And all of you"—he swung around on the group, holding them in place with his gaze—"are going to listen."

O

TWO

"You've told the story your way," Adam said. "Some of it's been close to the truth, and some of it's been just plain lies. But none of it happened exactly the way you told it."

He looked around the Circle again. "I don't care what you think of me," he said, "but there's somebody else involved here. And *she*"—he glanced at Cassie, just long enough for her to see his blue-gray eyes, still shining like silver—"doesn't deserve to be put through this, especially not tonight."

A few of the coven members, notably Laurel and Melanie, looked away, slightly ashamed. But the rest simply stared, angry and mistrustful.

"So what's your side of the story?" Deborah

said, scowling. Her expression said she felt she'd been taken in, and she didn't like it.

"First of all, it wasn't like that when Cassie and I met. It wasn't love at first sight . . ." Adam faltered for a moment, looking into the distance. He shook his head. "It wasn't love. She *helped* me, she saved me from four outsider guys with a gun. The witch-hunting kind of outsiders." He looked hard at Chris and Doug Henderson.

"But she didn't know—" Deborah began.

"She didn't know what I was, then. She didn't know what *she* was. Witches were something out of fairy tales to her. Cassie helped me just because I needed help. These guys were after me, and she stashed me in a boat and sent them all off running in the wrong direction down the beach. They tried to get her to tell where I was, they even hurt her, but she didn't give me up."

There was a silence. Deborah, who admired physical bravery above all other qualities, looked quizzical, her scowl smoothing out a little.

Faye, though, was squirming like a fish trying to get off a hook, and her expression was unpleasant. "How sweet. The brave heroine. So you just couldn't resist fooling around with her."

"Don't be a jerk, Faye," Adam said, giving Faye's arm a little shake. "I didn't do anything with her. We just—" He shook his head again. "I told her 'thank you.' I wanted her to know that I wouldn't forget what she'd done—remember, at the time I still thought she was an outsider, and I'd never known an outsider who did anything like that for one of us. She was just this nice outsider girl; sort of quiet and pretty, and I wanted to say 'thanks.' But when I was looking at her I suddenly felt—as if we were connected somehow. It sounds stupid now, maybe, but I could almost see this connection . . ."

"The silver cord," Cassie whispered. Her eyes were full, and she wasn't aware she'd spoken aloud until she saw faces swing toward her.

Melanie's eyebrows went up and Diana looked startled too, maybe just at hearing Cassie break the silence she'd kept so long. Suzan's rosebud lips were pursed into an O.

"Yeah, I guess that was what it looked like," Adam was saying, staring off into the distance again. "I don't know—it was just this confused impression. But I did feel grateful to her, and I would have liked her for a friend—how about that, an outsider friend?" There were murmurs of amusement and unbelief. "And," Adam said, looking straight at Diana, "that's why I gave her the chalcedony rose you gave me."

No murmurs this time. Grim silence.

"It was a token of friendship, a way to repay a debt," Adam said. "I figured if she ever got in trouble, I could sense it through the crystal and maybe do something to help. So I gave it to her—and that was *all* I did." He looked at Faye defiantly, and then even more defiantly around the group. "Except—yeah, right—I did kiss her. I kissed her hand."

Laurel blinked. The Henderson brothers looked at Adam sideways, as if to say he was crazy but they guessed it was his own business what bits of girls he kissed. Faye tried to look scornful, but it didn't come off very well.

"Then I left the Cape," Adam said. "I didn't see Cassie again until I came back up here for Kori's initiation—which turned out to be Cassie's initiation. But there's one other important thing. In all the time I talked to Cassie I never told her who I was or where I was from. I never told her my name. So whatever she came up here and did—whatever *poems* she wrote, Faye—she didn't know who I was. She didn't know Diana and I were together. Not until that night when I showed up on the beach."

16

"So I suppose that's a good reason for pretending you didn't know each other, for sneaking around behind everybody's back and meeting each other," Faye said, on the offensive again.

"You don't know what you're talking about," Adam said tightly, looking as if he'd like to shake Faye again. "We didn't sneak *anywhere*. The first time we ever talked alone was the night the skull ceremony in Diana's garage went wrong. Yeah, that night on the bluff when your little spies saw us, Faye. But d'you know what Cassie said to me in our first conversation alone since we'd met? She said she was in love with me—and that she knew it was wrong. Ever since she'd found out it was wrong, ever since she realized that I wasn't just some guy on the beach, but Diana's boyfriend, she'd been fighting against it. She'd even taken an oath—a blood oath—not to ever show anybody, by word or look or deed, how she felt about me. She didn't want Diana to find out and feel bad, or feel sorry for her. Does that sound like somebody who's trying to sneak around?"

The Circle looked back at him. Soberly, Melanie said, "Let me get this right. You're saying there's nothing at all to Faye's accusations?"

Adam swallowed. "No," he said quietly. "That's not what I'm saying. That night on the bluff . . ." He stopped and swallowed again, and then his voice hardened. "I can't explain what happened, except that it was my fault, not Cassie's. She did everything she could to avoid me, to keep out of my way. But once we were alone we were drawn together." He looked at Diana without flinching, although the pain was evident in his face. "I'm not proud of myself, but I never meant to hurt you. And Cassie is completely innocent. The only reason she was speaking to me at all that night was that she wanted to give me back the chalcedony rose—so I could give it back to you. In all of this, she's never been anything but honest and honorable. No matter what it cost her." He stopped and his mouth turned grim. "If I'd known she was being blackmailed by this snake—"

"I *beg* your pardon," Faye interrupted, golden eyes flashing dangerously.

Adam returned the look, just as dangerous. "That's what it was, wasn't it, Faye? Blackmail. Your little spies saw us that night—when we were saying *good-bye*, and swearing never to see each other alone again, and you decided to make the most of it. I knew there was something going on with you and Cassie after that, but I could never figure out what it was. Cassie was scared to death all of a sudden, but why she didn't just come to me and tell me what you were up to . . ." His voice trailed off and he looked toward Cassie.

Cassie shook her head mutely. How could she explain? "I didn't want you caught up in it too," she said in a voice scarcely above a whisper. "I was afraid you'd tell Diana, and Faye said if Diana found out . . ."

"What?" Adam said. When Cassie shook her head again he gave Faye's arm a little shake. "*What*, Faye! If Diana found out it would kill her? Wreck the coven? Is that what you told Cassie?"

Faye smirked. "If I did, it was only the truth, wasn't it? As things turned out." She wrenched away from Adam.

"So you used her love for Diana against her. You blackmailed her to make her help you find the skull, right? I'll bet it took some persuading."

Adam was only guessing, but his guess was dead on target. Cassie found herself nodding. "I found out where it was—"

"But *how?*" Diana interrupted, blurting it, speaking for the first time directly to Cassie. Cassie looked into the clear green eyes with the tears hanging on the dark lashes and spoke directly back.

"I did what Faye said," she said tremulously. "First I looked in the walnut cabinet—remember when I stayed overnight and you woke up with me in the room? When the skull wasn't there I thought I'd have to give up, but then I had a dream. It made me remember something I'd seen in your Book of Shadows, about purifying an evil object by burying it in sand. So I went and searched the beach and finally found the skull under that ring of stones."

Cassie paused, looking at Faye, her voice growing stronger. "Once I had my hands on it, though, I realized I *couldn't* give it to Faye. I just couldn't. But she had followed me and she took it anyway."

Cassie took a deep breath, making herself meet Diana's eyes again, her own eyes begging Diana to understand. "I know I shouldn't have let her have it. I should have stood up to her, then and afterward, but I was weak and stupid. I'm *sorry* now—I wish I'd just come and told you in the beginning, but I was so afraid you'd be

20

hurt . . ." Tears were choking her voice now, and making her vision blur. "And as for what Adam said—about it all being his fault—you have to know that isn't true. It was my fault, and at the Halloween dance I *tried* to make him kiss me, because I was so upset by then and I thought that nothing really mattered, since I was evil anyway."

There was wetness on Diana's cheeks, but now she looked taken aback. "Since *what?*"

"Since I was evil," Cassie said, hearing the terrible, stark truth in the simple words. "Since I was responsible for killing Jeffrey Lovejoy."

The entire coven stared at her, appalled.

"Wait a minute," Melanie said. "Run that by me one more time."

"Whenever anybody used the skull, it released dark energy, which went out and killed somebody," Cassie said carefully and clearly. "Faye and I were the ones who used the skull before Jeffrey was killed. If it wasn't for me, she couldn't have used it, and Jeffrey would still be alive. So, you see, I'm responsible."

Animation was returning to Diana's eyes. "But you didn't *know*," she said.

Cassie shook her head fiercely. "That's no excuse. There's no excuse for any of it—not even for doing worse things because I thought I was evil anyway and what did it matter? It *did* matter. I listened to Faye and I let her bully me." And I kept the hematite, she thought, but there was no point in getting into that. She shrugged, blinking more tears away. "I even let her make me vote for her for leader. I'm *sorry*, Diana—I'm so sorry. I don't know why I did it."

"I do," Diana said shakily. "Adam said it already—you were scared."

Cassie nodded. All the words she'd held back for so long were pouring out. "Once I started doing things for her, I couldn't stop. She had more and more to blackmail me with. Everything just went more and more wrong and I didn't know how to get out of it . . ." Cassie's voice broke. She saw Faye, lip curled, step forward and try to say something, and she saw Adam shut her up with a single glance. Then she turned and saw Diana's eyes.

They were as luminous as peridot crystals held up to the light, liquid with unshed tears, but also with—something else. It was a look Cassie had never expected to see again, especially not directed at *her*. A look of pain, yes, but also of forgiveness and longing. A look of love.

Something broke inside Cassie, something hard and tight that had been growing since she had started to deceive Diana. She took a stumbling step forward.

Then she and Diana were in each others' arms, both crying, both holding on with all their strength.

"I'm so sorry, I'm so sorry for everything," Cassie sobbed.

It seemed a long time before Diana drew back, and when she did she stepped away from the group, turning to look into the darkness. Cassie wiped her cheeks with the back of her hand. The moon, hanging low on the horizon, shone like old gold on Diana's hair.

There was absolute silence except for the distant roar and crash of waves on the beach. The entire group stood motionless, as if waiting for something that none of them could quite define.

At last Diana turned back to them. "I think we've all heard enough," she said. "I think I understand, maybe not everything, but most of it. Listen, everybody, because I don't want to say this again."

Everyone was quiet, their faces turned toward Diana expectantly. Cassie had the distinct feeling that a judgement was about to be rendered. Diana looked like a priestess or a princess, tall and pale, but resolute. There was a strange dignity about her, an aura of greatness and of certainty that belied the pain in her eyes.

I'm waiting to hear my punishment, Cassie thought. Whatever it was, she deserved it. She glanced at Adam and saw he was waiting too. His expression asked no favors, but Cassie knew what he must be feeling underneath it. They both stood before Diana, connected by their crime, glad to have it in the open at last.

"I don't want anybody to discuss what's happened tonight again," Diana said, her voice soft and distinct. "Not ever. Once I've finished talking we'll all consider the subject closed." She looked at Adam, not quite meeting his eyes. "I think," she said slowly, "that I know how it must have been for you. These things happen sometimes. I forgive you. And as for you, Cassie—you're even less to blame. There was no way for you to have known. I don't blame either of you. All I ask—"

Cassie drew a shuddering breath and broke in. She couldn't hold back any longer.

"Diana," she said, "I want you to know something. All this time, underneath, I've been angry and jealous because Adam belonged to you and not me. Even up until tonight. But all that's changed now—truly. Now all I want is for you and Adam to be happy. Nothing is more important to me than you—and the promise I made." For an instant it crossed Cassie's mind to wonder if Adam were *less* important, but she shoved the thought away and spoke earnestly, with utter conviction. "Adam and I—we both made that promise. If you'll just give us another chance to keep it—just one more chance . . ."

Diana was opening her mouth, but Cassie went on before she could speak.

"*Please*, Diana. You've got to know that you can trust me—that you can trust us. You've got to let us prove that."

There was a slight pause, then Diana said, "Yes. Yes—you're right." She took a deep breath and let it out, looking at Adam almost tentatively. "Well, then, what if—if we just forget all about this for a while? Just—wipe the slate clean?"

A muscle in Adam's jaw jerked. Silently, he took the hand Diana extended toward him.

Diana held her other hand out to Cassie. Cassie took it and held on tightly to the slim, cold fingers. She wanted to laugh and cry at

25

once. Instead she just gave Diana a wobbly smile. Looking at Adam she saw that he was trying to smile too, although his eyes were dark as storm clouds over the ocean.

"And that's *it*?" Faye exploded. "Everything's all right now, all sweetness and light? Everybody loves everybody and you're all going home holding hands?"

"Yes," Adam snapped, giving her a hard look. "As for the last, anyway. We're going home—it's past time for that."

"Cassie needs to rest," Diana agreed. The blank helplessness had left her entirely, and although she looked more fragile than Cassie had ever seen her before, she also looked determined. "We all need that."

"And we need to call a doctor—or somebody," Deborah said unexpectedly. She inclined her head toward Number Twelve. "Cassie's grandma . . ."

"Whose side are you on?" Faye snarled. Deborah just gave her a cool look.

Diana's fingers tightened on Cassie's. "Yes. You're right, we'll call Dr. Stern—and Cassie can come home with me."

Faye gave a short bark of laughter, but nobody laughed with her. Even the Henderson brothers

26

were serious, their slanted eyes thoughtful. Suzan twisted a lock of strawberry-blond hair around her fingers, looking at Cassie's and Diana's intertwined hands. Laurel nodded encouragingly when Cassie glanced at her, and Melanie's cool gray eyes shone with quiet approval. Sean chewed his lip, looking uncertainly from one member of the group to another.

But it was Nick's expression that surprised Cassie most. His face, usually so unemotional, was clearly strained, as if there were some violent struggle going on beneath the surface.

There was no time to think about him now, though. No time even to think about Faye, who was seething uselessly, her plans to fracture the coven in ruins. Melanie was speaking.

"Do you want to go by my house first, Cassie? Great-aunt Constance is looking after your mom, and if you want to see her . . ."

Cassie nodded eagerly. It seemed like a hundred years since she had seen her mother, since she had been inside that room filled with red light, looking at her mother's glassy, empty eyes. Surely her mother would be all right by now; surely she would be able to tell Cassie what had happened.

But when the three of them, Melanie, Cassie, and Diana, who hadn't let go of Cassie's hand on the short drive to Number Four, went into the house, Cassie's heart sank. Melanie's great-aunt, a thin-lipped woman with severe eyes, led them silently into a downstairs guest room. One look at the ghostly figure on the bed sent chills of dismay through Cassie's bloodstream.

"Mom?" she whispered, knowing already there would be no answer.

God, her mother looked *young*. Even younger than she normally did, frighteningly young, unnaturally so. It was as if it weren't Cassie's mother on the bed there at all, but some little girl with dark hair and big haunted black eyes that vaguely resembled Mrs. Blake's. A stranger.

Not someone who was going to be of help to Cassie.

"It's okay, Mom," Cassie whispered, stepping away from Diana to put a hand on her mother's shoulder. "Everything's going to be all right. You'll see. You're going to be just fine."

Her throat ached, and then she felt Diana gently leading her away.

"You've both been through enough," Melanie said once they were outside again. "Let us take care of things with the doctor—and the police, if they have to come. You and Cassie get some sleep."

The rest of the coven was waiting in the street, and they nodded in agreement when Melanie said this. Cassie looked at Diana, who nodded too.

"Okay," Cassie said. It came out faint and slightly hoarse and she realized how tired she was—bone-tired. At the same time she was light-headed, and the entire scene in front of her was assuming a dreamlike quality. It was just too strange to be standing out here in the wee hours of the morning, knowing that her grandmother was dead and her mother was in shock, and that she didn't have a house to go back to. Yet there were no adults on the street, no commotion, only the members of the Circle and an eerie stillness. Come to think of it, why *weren't* there any parents out here? Surely some of them must have heard what was going on.

But the houses on Crowhaven Road remained shuttered and silent. On the way to Melanie's house, Cassie thought she'd seen a light go off in Suzan's house and a curtain whisk back at the Henderson's. If any adults were awake, they weren't getting involved.

We're on our own, Cassie thought. But Diana was beside her, and she could see Adam's tall form silhouetted against the headlights of the coven's parked cars. A sort of strength flowed into Cassie just at their nearness.

"We've got to talk tomorrow," she said. "There's a lot I've got to tell you—all of you. Things my grandmother told me right before . . . before she died."

"We can meet at lunchtime on the beach—" Diana began, but Faye's throaty voice cut her off.

"No, we can't. *I'm* the one who decides where the meetings are now, or had you forgotten?"

Faye's head was thrown back proudly, the silver crescent-moon diadem gleaming against the midnight-black of her hair. Diana opened her mouth, then shut it again.

"All right," Adam said with deceptive calmness, stepping out of the glare of headlights to stand by Faye. "You're the leader. So lead. Where do we meet?"

Faye's eyes narrowed. "At the old science building. But—"

"Fine." Adam didn't wait for her to finish; he turned his back on her. "I'll drive you home," he said to Diana and Cassie.

Faye looked furious, but the three of them were already moving away. "By the way, Diana—happy birthday," she called spitefully after them.

Diana didn't answer.

THREE

"Jacinth! Are you in there? Jacinth!"

Cassie blinked in the bright sunlight. She'd
seen this room before. It was her grandmother's
kitchen—except that it wasn't. The walls of her
grandmother's kitchen were sagging and dingy;
these were straight and clean. Her grandmother's
hearth was stained with the smoke of centuries;
this hearth looked almost new and was a slightly
different shape. The iron hook for hanging pots
on shone.

It was the room in her dream, the dream she'd
had the last time she spent the night at Diana's
house. The low chair she was sitting in was the
same. But this dream seemed to be picking up
where the other had left off.

"Jacinth, have you fallen asleep with your eyes open? Kate is here!"

A feeling of anticipation and excitement filled Cassie. Kate; who was Kate? Without even knowing why, she found herself standing up, and she realized that she was wearing a dress that brushed the tips of her neat brocade shoes. The red leather Book of Shadows fell from her lap to the ground.

She turned toward the voice, toward what would have been the side door of her grandmother's house. In this house it seemed to be the front door. It was filled with sunlight, and there were two figures standing there. One was tall, with a silhouette like the engravings of Puritan women she'd seen in history books. The other was smaller, with shining hair.

Cassie couldn't see either of the figures' faces, but the smaller one was holding out eager hands to her. Cassie reached for them, stepping forward—

—and the dream changed. It was dark and she could hear the tortured scream of wood being ripped asunder. Salt spray stung her face and her eyes struggled vainly to pierce the darkness.

The ship was going down. Lost, all lost. And the Master Tools were lost as well—for now.

But only for now. The savage determination of the thought filled Cassie and she tasted bile at the back of her throat. Even as icy water rushed around her legs she felt the dream lose focus. She tried to hang on to it, but it melted and shifted around her, and the darkness of the turbulent, stormy night became the quiet darkness of Diana's room.

She was awake.

And relieved beyond reason just to be alive.

It wasn't really so dark in here. Dawn was brightening the curtains, turning the room gray. Diana was sleeping peacefully beside her. How *could* Diana be peaceful after all that had happened? After what Diana had learned about her best friend and her boyfriend, after losing the leadership of the coven, how could Diana sleep at all? But the dark lashes on Diana's cheek were still and serene and there was no bitterness in Diana's face.

She's so good. I could never be that good, Cassie thought. Not if I tried all my life. Still, just being near Diana made her feel better.

Cassie knew she wasn't going to sleep anymore. She sat back against the headboard and thought.

God, she was glad to have things right with

Diana again. And with Adam—Cassie was almost afraid to think of Adam, worried about what kind of pain it would bring. But although there was a deep-down ache at the picture of him, it was not unbearable, and the poison of jealousy and anger was truly gone. She honestly wanted him and Diana to be happy. She was a different person from the one who'd burned with the frustration of not being able to have him these last six weeks.

She'd done a lot of strange things in the last six weeks, so many that she hardly knew herself anymore. I can't believe it, she thought; I went out and stole pumpkins with Chris and Doug in Salem. I drove that dog off Chris—that wasn't like me at all. I played Pizza Man with Faye. I went on that wild motorcycle ride with Deborah . . . well, that wasn't so bad.

A lot of things she'd done in the last month weren't all bad. The lying and deception and guilt had been awful, but some of the changes had been good. She'd gotten closer to Deborah and Suzan, and she'd gained some insight into what made the Henderson brothers tick. Even Nick—she thought she understood him better now. And she'd found strength in herself she'd never thought she had. Strength to chase the shadowy thing in the cemetery—Black John?—after Jeffrey's death, strength to ask a boy to a dance, strength, in the end, to stand up to Faye.

She only hoped it was enough strength to stand up to the days ahead.

Cassie hadn't been to the old science building since Faye had lured her there and held her hostage, that first week of school. It was just as dark and unsafe-looking as she remembered. She had no idea why Faye had wanted them to meet here, except that this was Faye's territory, while the beach had always been Diana's.

It was strange to see Faye in Diana's place, standing in front of the group with all eyes on her. Faye was wearing ordinary clothes today, black leggings and a red and black striped sweater, but a mysterious aura of leadership still clung to her. As she paced, her star rubies flashed in the shafts of sunlight that came through the boarded-up windows.

"I believe it was Cassie who wanted this meeting called. She said there was a lot she had to tell us—right, Cassie?"

"About what my grandmother said before she died," Cassie said steadily, looking Faye in the eyes. "Before Black John killed her." If she'd expected Faye to be abashed, she was disappointed; those hooded golden eyes remained level and arrogant. Apparently Faye took no responsibility for the actions of Black John, even though she was the one who'd arranged for him to be set free.

"Was it really Black John?" Suzan said doubtfully, putting a exquisitely manicured fingernail to her perfect mouth, as if thinking was a new and difficult exercise. "Was he really there?"

"He was really there. He *is* really *here*," Cassie said. Suzan wasn't as stupid as she acted, and sometimes she had surprising insights. Cassie wanted her on their side. "He came out of that mound in the cemetery. It was his grave, I guess. When we brought the skull to the cemetery and released the dark energy, it gave him the strength to come back."

"Back from the dead?" Sean asked nervously.

Before Cassie could answer, Melanie said, "That mound couldn't have been Black John's grave, Cassie. I'm sorry, but it just couldn't. It's far too modern."

"I know it's modern. It's not Black John's first grave; I don't even know if he had a grave in the 1600s. I guess not if he died at sea . . ." There were startled looks from some of the group, but Cassie scarcely noticed. "Anyway, it's not his grave from then. It's his grave from 1976."

Laurel, who was pouring a thermos cup of herbal tea, sloshed hot liquid on the floor.

Faye stopped dead. *What?* she snarled.

Even Diana and Adam looked disconcerted, glancing at each other. But support came from an unexpected quarter.

"Just let her tell the story," Deborah said. Thumbs hooked in her jeans pockets, she moved to where Cassie was sitting on an overturned crate, and stood beside her.

Cassie took a deep breath. "I knew something was weird when I saw all those graves in the cemetery—graves of *your* parents, all killed in 1976. Diana said it was a hurricane, but it still seemed strange to me. I mean, why were only parents dead? Especially when I learned that you'd all been born just a few months before. With all those little babies, you'd think some of them would have died in an ordinary hurricane. That's not even to mention the weirdness of *all* of you being born within a one-month period."

She was relaxing a little now, although it was difficult to talk with everyone looking at her. At least their eyes weren't glinting with enmity and suspicion today. Only Faye looked hostile, standing with her arms folded across her chest, her feline eyes narrowed.

"But you see, the explanation for all of it is really simple," Cassie went on. "Black John came back during the last generation, our parents' generation. Nobody knew it was him, and my grandmother said nobody could ever figure out how he came back, but it was Black John. He tried to make our parents into a coven when they were just a little older than us."

"*Our* parents?" Doug asked, snickering. "C'mon, Cassie, give us a break." There were chuckles from others in the audience, and the expressions ranged from skeptical to troubled to openly mocking.

"No, wait," Adam said, beginning to look excited. "There are some things that that would explain. I know my grandmother wanders in her mind now and then, but she's said things to me about my parents—about us kids forming a coven—that just might fit." His blue-gray eyes were snapping with intensity.

"Here's something else," Deborah said, looking sideways at Nick. "Cassie's grandma said my mom was going to marry Nick's dad, but Black John made her marry my dad instead. That might explain why my mom freaks when you even mention magic, and why she always looks kind of guilty when she says Nick is growing up to look just like his father. It might explain a lot."

Cassie noticed Nick, who was standing apart from the group as usual, in a dark corner. He was staring at the floor so hard, his eyes seemed to be about to bore a hole through it. "Yeah, it might," he said so softly Cassie could barely hear the words. She wondered what he meant.

"It would explain why they yell at each other all the time, too—my parents, I mean," Deborah was adding.

"All parents yell all the time," Chris said with a shrug.

"All the parents around *here* are the ones who survived Black John," said Cassie. "They survived because they didn't go to fight him. My grandmother said that after eleven babies were born in one month, our parents realized what Black John was up to. He wanted a coven he could control completely, a coven of *kids* he could mold while they were growing up. You guys"—Cassie nodded around the group—"were going to be his coven."

The members of the Club looked at one

another. "But what about you, Cassie?" Laurel asked.

"I wasn't born until later. Neither was Kori, you know. We weren't part of Black John's plans; we were just regular kids. But you guys were going to be *his*. He arranged everything about you."

"And the parents who didn't like that idea went to fight Black John," Deborah put in. "They killed him; they burned him and the house at Number Thirteen, but they died themselves doing it. The ones that are alive are the cowards who stayed at home."

"Like *my* father," Suzan said abruptly, looking up from her nails. "He gets really nervous if you mention the Vietnam Memorial or the Titanic or anything about anybody dying to save other people. And he won't talk about my mom."

Cassie saw startled looks around the Circle. There was a kind of recognition in many of the members' eyes.

"Like *my* dad," Diana said wonderingly. "He always talks about my mother being so brave, but he's never said exactly why. No wonder, if he didn't go, if he let her go alone." She bit her lip, distressed. "What a horrible thing to find out about your own father."

"Yeah, well, I've got it worse," Deborah said, looking grim. "*Both* my parents didn't go. And neither did yours," she added to the Hendersons, who looked at each other and scowled.

"While those of us with no parents are lucky?" Melanie asked, raising her eyebrows.

"At least you know they had guts," Deborah said shortly. "You and Adam and Laurel and Nick have something to be proud of. I'd rather be raised by a grandmother or a great-aunt than have parents who scream at each other all the time because they're so ashamed of themselves."

Cassie was watching Nick again, and she saw something leave his face, some tension that had been there ever since she'd known him. It made him look different, softer somehow, more vulnerable. At that moment he raised his eyes and met hers, catching her in the act of watching him. Cassie wanted to look away, but she couldn't, and to her surprise there was no hostility in his gaze. His mouth crooked slightly in a wry, relieved smile, and she found herself almost smiling back in sympathy.

Then she realized Faye was looking at them. Turning back, she spoke quickly to the entire group.

"The ones who died were killed because our

parents didn't all stick together. That's what my grandmother said, anyway. She said that *we* were the ones in danger now, because Black John's come to take us back. He still wants his coven, and now he's alive again—a living, breathing man. She said that he won't look burned and awful when we see him again, and we might not recognize him, but we have to be ready for him."

"Why?" Adam asked, his level voice seeming loud in the sudden silence. "Just what did she think he's going to do?"

Cassie lifted her hands. There was no longer a guilty secret between her and Adam, but every time she looked at him, she felt—a connection. A new connection, that of two people who'd been tried by fire and had come out stronger. There would always be an understanding between them.

"I don't know what he's going to do," she told Adam. "Fool us, my grandma said. Get us to follow him the way our parents did. But *how*, I don't know."

"The reason I ask is because he may not want *all* of us," Adam said, still quietly. "You said he arranged for the eleven of us to be born—and if he joins the coven as its leader, that makes twelve. But you weren't one of the eleven,

Cassie. Neither was Kori. And it looks like he got Kori out of the way."

Diana drew in a sharp breath. "Oh, my God—Cassie! You've got to leave. You've got to get out of New Salem, go back to California—" She stopped, because Cassie was shaking her head.

"I can't," Cassie said simply. "My grandma told me I had to stay and fight. She said that was why my mom brought me back, so I *could* fight him. I may be half outsider, but I guess I'm one kid he didn't plan, so maybe I have some kind of advantage."

"Don't be modest," Deborah broke in caustically. "The old lady told us it was because your family was always the strongest. You've got the clearest sight and the most power, she said."

"And I've got our Book of Shadows, now," Cassie said, somewhat embarrassed, bending to take the red leather book out of her backpack. "My grandmother had it hidden behind a loose brick in the kitchen fireplace. Black John wanted it, so there must be something in it that he's afraid of. I'm going to read it and try to find out what that something is."

"What can the rest of us do?" Laurel asked. Cassie realized the question was directed at *her*; except for Faye, who was glowering, they were all

45

looking at her expectantly. Flustered, she lifted her hands again and shook her head.

"We can talk to the old ladies in the town who're still alive," Deborah suggested. "That's my idea, anyway. Cassie's grandma said our parents have forgotten about magic, that they made themselves forget to survive. But I figure the old ladies might not have forgotten, and we can question them. Like Laurel's Granny Quincey, and Adam's grandma, old Mrs. Franklin. Even your great-aunt, Mel."

Melanie looked doubtful. "Great-aunt Constance doesn't approve of the old ways *at all*. She's pretty—inflexible—about it."

"And Granny Quincey is so frail," Laurel said. "As for old Mrs. Franklin—well, she's not always all there."

"To put it tactfully," Adam said. "Let's face it, my grandmother can get pretty loopy at times. But I think Deborah's right; they're all we've got, so we have to make the most of them. We can *try* to pump some parents for information, too . . . what have we got to lose?"

"An arm and an eye, if it's my father you're pumping," Suzan muttered, holding her fingers in a shaft of sunlight to examine her nails. But Chris and Doug Henderson grinned wildly and said they'd be happy to interrogate all the parents.

"We'll say, 'Hey, remember that guy you fried like Freddy Krueger sixteen years ago? Well, he's back, so can you, like, give us any help in recognizing him?'" Doug said with relish.

"Didn't your grandma say *anything* that might help?" Laurel asked Cassie.

"No . . . wait." Cassie straightened up, excitement stirring inside her. "She said they identified Black John's body in the burned house because of his ring, a lodestone ring." She looked at Melanie. "You're the crystal expert; so what's lodestone?"

"It's magnetite, black iron oxide," Melanie said, her cool gray eyes narrowed thoughtfully. "It's like hematite, which is iron oxide too, but hematite's blood-red when you cut it in thin slices. Magnetite is black and magnetic."

Cassie tried to control her expression. Well, she'd known the hematite came from Black John's house; maybe it had even been his stone. She shouldn't be surprised that he wore a ring of something similar. Still, she felt a twinge of apprehension. She'd really better get rid of that piece of hematite. Right now it was sitting in a jewelry box in her bedroom, where she'd put it when Diana drove her over to her house to pick up her clothes this morning before school.

"Okay, we'll keep on the lookout for that," Adam was saying, sparing Cassie the necessity of speaking. "We can talk to the old ladies tomorrow—or maybe we should wait until after Cassie's grandmother's funeral."

"All right," Cassie murmured.

"You're making a lot of *suggestions*, Adam," Faye said, stung into speaking at last. Her arms were still folded over her chest, and her honey-pale skin was flushed with anger.

Adam looked back without expression. "Come to think of it, there was another suggestion I was going to make," he said. "I think we should retake the leadership vote."

Faye lunged toward him, golden eyes blazing. "You can't do that!"

"Why not? If all of us agree," Adam said calmly.

"Because it's not in the traditions," Faye hissed. "You look at any Book of Shadows and you'll see! The vote is the vote; I won and it can't be changed now. *I'm* the coven leader."

Adam turned to the others for help, but Melanie was looking troubled and Diana was slowly shaking her head.

"She's right, Adam," Diana said softly. "The vote was fair, at the time. There aren't any provisions for changing it." Melanie nodded her unwilling agreement.

"And I don't like you making all these plans without consulting me," Faye went on, pacing again like a panther in a cage. Sparks actually seemed to flash from her eyes, the way they flashed from the red gems at her throat and on her fingers as she crossed patches of sunlight.

"Well, what do *you* want us to do?" Laurel said challengingly, tossing her long light-brown hair back. "You were the one who wanted Black John out, Faye. You said he was going to help us, to give us his power. Well, how about it? What do you say now that he's here?"

Faye was breathing hard. "He may be testing us—"

"By killing Cassie's grandma?" Deborah cut in harshly. "Don't be stupid, Faye. I was there; I *saw* it. There's no excuse for murdering old ladies."

Faye glared at her defecting ex-lieutenant. "I don't know why he did that! Maybe he has some plans that we don't know about."

"*That's* the truest thing you've ever said," Melanie interrupted. "He does have plans,

Faye—to take us over. He's already killed four people, and if we annoy him I'm sure he'll be happy to kill us, too."

Faye stopped pacing and smiled triumphantly. "He can't," she snapped. "If Cassie is right—and I'm not saying she is, but *if* she is—then he needs us for his coven. So he can't kill us!"

"Well, he can't kill all of us, anyway," Adam said dryly. "He can only spare one."

Silence fell. The members of the Circle glanced uneasily at one another.

"Well, then, maybe you'd each better be sure *you're* not the one," Faye said, smiling around at them. It wasn't quite her old, lazy smile; it was more a baring of teeth. Before anyone could say anything she turned around and stalked out of the room. They could hear her footsteps going rapidly down the stairs, then the slam of the science building's front door.

Cassie, Adam, and Diana looked at one another. Adam shook his head.

"We're in trouble," he said.

"Oh, so is that what we figured out at this meeting?" said Deborah.

Diana leaned her forehead against her hand wearily. "We need her," she said. "She *is* the coven leader, and we need her on our side, not

50

on his. We'd better go talk to her."

Slowly, the Club members got up. Outside, it was too bright, and Cassie squinted. Seventh period had just ended and people were flooding out of the school exits. Cassie scanned the crowds but couldn't see Faye.

"She's probably gone home," Diana was saying. "We'll have to go after her . . ."

Cassie didn't hear the rest. Among the milling students in the parking lot she had suddenly glimpsed a familiar face. A *strange* familiar face, one that didn't belong here, one that she had to rack her brains to identify. For God's sake, where had she seen that turned-up nose, that straw-colored hair, those cold hazel eyes before? It was someone she'd known quite well, someone she'd been used to looking at day after day, but that she'd been only too happy to forget about when she came to New Salem.

A feeling of heat and humidity overcame Cassie. A memory of sand underfoot, sweat trickling down her sides, suntan lotion greasy on her nose. A sound of lapping waves and a smell of overheated bodies and a sense of oppression.

Cape Cod.

The familiar girl was Portia.

FOUR

"Hey, watch out, Cassie," Chris said, running into her as she stopped in her tracks. "What's wrong?"

"I just saw someone." Cassie could feel how wide her eyes were as she stared into the crowd. Portia had disappeared in a sea of bobbing heads. "A girl I knew this summer . . ." Her voice trailed off as her mind boggled at the task of explaining Portia to the Circle.

But Adam had seen her too. "A witch hunter," he said grimly. "The one whose brothers carried a gun. They're seriously into it—not just as a hobby, but as an obsession."

"And they've come *here*?" Deborah scoffed. Cassie looked back and forth between the dark-haired girl and Adam; obviously witch-hunting was something these people had encountered before. "They ought to know better."

"Maybe it was a mistake—or an accident. Maybe her parents moved and she was just transferred here or something," Laurel said, ever the optimist.

Cassie shook her head. "Portia doesn't make mistakes," she murmured. "And I pity the accident that tries to happen to her. Adam, what are we going to do?" She was almost more upset by this than she had been by the knowledge that Black John was loose somewhere in New Salem. *That* terror was mind-numbing, too much to deal with rationally. Fear of Portia was more familiar, and Cassie felt herself being sucked toward an old pattern of helplessness. She'd never been able to deal with Portia; she came out of every encounter tongue-tied and humiliated, defeated. Cassie shut her eyes.

I am not like that anymore. I won't *be* like that, she thought. But dread churned in her stomach.

"We'll deal with her," Adam was beginning bleakly when Doug leaned in, his tilted blue-green eyes sparkling.

"Hey, she's an enemy, right? Black John the

Witch Dude said he wanted to help us destroy our enemies, right? So—"

"Don't even think about it," Melanie cut in swiftly. "*Don't*, Doug. I mean it."

Doug hunched his shoulders, but he looked at his twin sideways under his lashes.

"Bad magic," Chris muttered, staring into the distance.

Cassie looked at Adam.

"Never," Adam said reassuringly. "Don't worry, Cassie. Never."

Cassie was living with Diana now. "Obviously you can't stay in that house alone," Diana had said, and that afternoon she and Laurel and Melanie helped Cassie move her things. Adam and Deborah came too, for protection, pacing around the house restlessly, and most of the other Club members stopped by for one reason or another. Only Faye was conspicuously absent. No one had seen her since she'd disappeared from school.

The house itself wasn't too badly damaged, aside from the strange burned places on the floor and some of the doors. The official story, as decided on by the adults who'd come last night to take Cassie's grandmother's body away, was that there had been a fire and Mrs. Howard had been frightened into a heart attack. The Club hadn't mentioned an intruder, and the police hadn't even cordoned the house off. How the police thought a hardwood floor had caught fire in such a strange pattern, Cassie didn't know. Nobody had asked her and she certainly wasn't going down to the station to volunteer anything.

The house seemed empty and echoing despite the Circle members bustling around it. There was an emptiness inside Cassie, too. She'd never have thought she would miss her grandmother so much—just a stooped old lady with coarse gray hair and a mole on her cheek. But those old eyes had seen a lot, and those knotted hands had been deft and kind. Her grandmother had *known* things, and she had always made Cassie feel better.

"I wish I had a picture of her," Cassie said softly. "My grandma." Witches didn't like being photographed, so she didn't even have that.

"She was a pretty cool old broad," Deborah said, slinging a tote bag over one shoulder and picking up a cardboard box full of books and CDs. "You want anything else?"

Cassie looked around the room. Yes, everything, she thought. She wanted her four-poster bed with the dusty-rose canopy and hangings, and her damask-upholstered chairs, and her solid mahogany chest that was just the color of Nick's eyes.

"That's bombé, that chest of drawers there," she told Deborah. "It was made here in Massachusetts, the only place in the colonies that produced that style."

"Yeah, I know," Deborah said, unimpressed. "My house is full of it. It weighs a ton and you can't take it. You want the stereo, or what?"

"No, I can use Diana's," Cassie said sadly. She felt as if she were leaving her life behind. I'm only moving down the road, she reminded herself as Deborah left.

"Cassie, if you want to stop by and see your mom this afternoon, it's okay with Great-aunt Constance," Melanie said, appearing in the doorway. "Any time before dinner."

Cassie nodded, feeling something twist in her chest. Her mother. Of course her mom was going to be all right; Melanie's great-aunt was willing to take care of her, and it would be better for her to stay at Melanie's house than to be taken—somewhere else. Say what you mean: an institution, she told herself fiercely. If the doctors saw her they'd want to put her in an institution or a hospital. But she doesn't belong there, and she's going to be just fine. She needs to rest a little, that's all.

"Thanks, Melanie," she said. "I'll come after we finish moving. It's nice of your aunt to take care of her."

"With Great-aunt Constance it's not so much nice; it's duty," Melanie said, turning to go. "Great-aunt Constance believes in doing your duty."

So do I, Cassie thought, pausing as she picked up a bundle of clothes from the bed. So do I. "I just thought of something—I'll be down in a second," she said.

What she'd thought of was the hematite. One-handed, she opened the jewelry box on the dresser—and then stiffened. She stirred through the contents of the box with her fingers, but it was no use.

The piece of hematite was gone.

Panic swelled in Cassie's throat. She'd kept *meaning* to do something about the stone, but now that it was out of her hands she realized how dangerous she thought it really was.

This time, she told herself, you are not going to keep it a secret and worry and stew about it all by yourself. This time you're going to do what you should have done in the beginning, which is tell Diana.

Cassie went downstairs. Diana and Laurel were in the herb garden, salvaging things Laurel thought might be useful. Cassie squared her shoulders.

"Diana," she said, "I've got something to tell you."

Diana's green eyes widened when Cassie explained about the hematite, how she'd found it, how she'd kept it a secret. No one had known about it except Deborah—and Faye.

"And now it's gone," Cassie said. "I don't think that means anything good."

"No," Diana said slowly. "I'm sure it doesn't. Cassie, don't you see, when you were carrying the hematite, it affected you. It made you do things . . . were you wearing it at the Halloween dance when you tried to make Adam kiss you?"

"I . . . yes." Cassie could feel the blood rising to her cheeks. "But, Diana—I wish I could say the hematite made me do that, but it *didn't*. It was just me. I wanted to."

"Maybe, but I'll bet you'd wanted to before and you didn't actually do it. Hematite might not force you to do things against your will, but it makes it easier to give in to things you normally wouldn't."

"Like onyx. Surrender to your shadow-self," Cassie whispered.

"Yes," said Diana.

"It must be one of us who has it; one of the Circle," Cassie said. "Because I put it in the box this morning and nobody else has been by the house today. But *which* one of us?"

Diana shook her head. Laurel grimaced. "I stick to plants," she said. "They're safer, as long as you respect them and know what you're doing. They don't influence you."

At Diana's suggestion, the three of them searched Cassie's room again. But the hematite was nowhere to be found.

Cassie went to school on Thursday. It was strange to sit in her writing class and see life going on around her as usual. All these people—students counting the days until Thanksgiving vacation, teachers giving their lectures, the vice-principal walking through the halls and looking harried—had no idea what was loose in their community, just waiting to strike again. Of course, Cassie didn't know exactly, either. What form was Black John going to take now? What would he look like when she saw him next? But she knew there was danger.

Faye didn't show up for English. Cassie had to stay after class to explain to Mr. Humphries why she'd been absent for two days. He was sympathetic and told her to take extra time for her next assignment, but it was hard to get away from him. Cassie was already late for algebra when she hurried into the third-floor bathroom. But once in a stall, she heard voices outside that made her freeze and forget the time.

They were carrying on a conversation that had obviously been going for a while.

"And then she was supposed to go back to California," the first voice was saying. Cassie had heard it too many times not to recognize it. Portia. "But that was obviously a lie too, if it's the same Cassie I knew."

"What did you say she looked like?" asked the other voice. A strident, contentious voice. Cassie recognized Sally Waltman.

"Oh, she's just a little nonentity. She's completely average, average height, a little taller than you . . ."

A throat-clearing sound from Sally.

"Not that you're *short*, of course. You're— petite. Anyway, she's got a fairly slim build, and everything about her is just ordinary: ordinary brownish hair, ordinary little face, ordinary clothes—*not* anything to write home about. Overall, she's unutterably dreary—"

"It's not the same Cassie," Sally interrupted curtly. "This one had every guy at Homecoming dance following her around with his tongue hanging out. Including *my* boyfriend—and look where it got him. She looks ordinary at first, maybe, but there are all sorts of colors in her hair; it changes depending on the light. I'm serious. And I'm sure it's just an act, but she's the kind that looks all fragile and sweet, the kind guys are just dying to take care of—and *then* she starts ordering them around. And she gets away with it, probably because she opens those great big eyes and pretends she thinks she's inadequate. The 'Oh, I'm just the girl next door, but I'll do my *best*' routine—they lap it up."

Cassie opened her mouth indignantly, then closed it again.

"And she's got eyes to kill for," Sally was going on bitterly. "Not the color, so much—they're sort of grayish blue—but they're so big and *sincere* it's disgusting. They always look like they're full of tears just ready to spill. Drives the guys crazy."

"It *is* the same girl," Portia said positively.

"Only when I knew her she had the sense not to flaunt herself. She knew her place then."

"Well, right now her place is with the most popular clique in school. They all think they're so wonderful; they think they can do anything. Including kill people."

"Well, not anymore," Portia said with satisfaction. "Things around here are about to change dramatically—for the better. You know, I'm *glad* my mom decided to move here after the divorce. I thought it would be terrible, but it's all turning out for the best."

Cassie held herself carefully still. So Sally and Portia were joining forces. Now if they would just be so obliging as to describe a little of their plans . . .

But the sound of running water drowned out the next few sentences, and then she heard Sally say, "I'd better get to calculus. Want to meet for lunch?"

"Yes, and I think you should come over to my house at Thanksgiving vacation," Portia said. "I think you'll like my brothers."

Cassie stood protectively surrounded by the rest of the Circle. It was Saturday and the burial was almost over.

This wasn't the old burying ground, the one which had been "vandalized" (that was the official story) the night her grandmother died. It was the modern cemetery where Kori had been buried. Modern in New Salem terms, that is: the oldest graves were from the 1800s. Cassie wondered why the parents killed by Black John in 1976 hadn't been buried here. Maybe someone had felt the old graveyard was more appropriate.

People were coming up to her, saying how sorry they were, asking about her mother. The official story on her mother was that she was in shock over the death of Cassie's grandmother and too ill to come. Cassie told them her mother was going to be fine.

Faye had showed up, to Cassie's surprise. Her lacy black dress was beautiful, if a little too clinging to be appropriate at a funeral. Her red lips and nails were the only touches of color about her.

"So sorry," a familiar voice said coolly, and Cassie looked up to see Portia. Sally was right behind her; those two seemed joined at the hip these days.

"What a surprise to see you here," Portia added, her hazel eyes fixed on Cassie's. Cassie remembered them; mean as snake's eyes, she thought. They seemed to have a mesmerizing effect, and Cassie felt the crushing sense of helplessness start to descend.

She fought it, and tried to speak, but Portia was going on. "I didn't realize you had family up here. But maybe now that you don't you'll be going back to California . . . ?"

"No, I'm staying." To Cassie's frustration, she couldn't think of anything else to say. She'd come up with a devastatingly witty retort tonight, undoubtedly.

But she wasn't alone in New Salem. Adam said, "Cassie still has family here," and moved to Cassie's side.

"Yeah, we're all brothers. All life is, like, linked," Chris said, coming up on Cassie's other side. He stared at Portia out of his strange blue-green eyes. Doug joined him, grinning his mad grin.

Portia blinked. Cassie had forgotten what the Henderson brothers looked like to people who didn't know them.

But Portia recovered quickly. "That's right—they say all you people are related. Well, maybe someday soon you'll meet *my* family." She looked at Adam. "I'm sure they'd enjoy that."

She turned on her heel and walked away.

Cassie and Adam exchanged a glance, but before they could say anything, Mr. Humphries had stepped up.

"It's been a beautiful service," he told Cassie. "We'll all miss your grandmother."

"Thank you," Cassie said. She managed a smile for him; she liked Mr. Humphries, with his neat little salt-and-pepper beard and his sympathetic eyes behind gold-rimmed glasses. "It was nice of you to come."

"I hope your mother is feeling better soon," said Mr. Humphries, and then he moved on. Ms. Lanning, Cassie's American-history teacher, came up to talk then, but Cassie's attention lingered on Mr. Humphries. A tall man with dark hair had joined him, and Cassie heard the rumble of a deep voice, followed by Mr. Humphries's lighter, quicker tones.

"—introduce me?" the dark man was saying.

"Why, certainly," Mr. Humphries said. He turned back to Cassie, bringing the dark man with him. "Cassie, I thought you might want to meet our new principal, Mr. Jack Brunswick. He's interested in getting to know his students as soon as possible."

"That's right," the tall man said, in deep,

pleasant tones. He reached out and took Cassie's hand in a firm grip. His own hand was large and strong. She glanced down at it as she opened her mouth to say something polite, but then froze, paralyzed, feeling her heart pound like a trip-hammer while the blood drained out of her face.

"I don't think she's feeling well—this must have been a long day—" Ms. Lanning was saying, but her voice seemed to come from a distance. She took hold of Cassie's arm.

But Cassie couldn't let go of the dark man's hand with its strong, well-made fingers. All she could see was the signet ring on his index finger, carved with a symbol that reminded her of the inscriptions on Diana's silver bracelet—Faye's silver bracelet now. The stone in the ring was black and reflective, with a metallic luster. It looked like hematite, but Cassie knew it wasn't. It was a lodestone.

Then, at last, Cassie looked up at the new principal, and she saw the face she'd seen during the skull ceremony in Diana's garage. The face that had rushed at her, faster and faster, bigger and bigger, trying to escape from the crystal skull. A cruel, cold face. For an instant she seemed to see the crystal skull itself superimposed on the principal's face, its bone structure clearly visible. The hollow eyes, the grinning teeth—

Cassie swayed on her feet. Ms. Lanning was trying to support her; she could hear Adam's alarmed voice, and Diana's. But she could see nothing except the darkness of the new principal's eyes. They were like glassy volcanic rock, like the ocean at midnight, like magnetite. They were swallowing her up. . . .

Cassie. The voice was in her mind.

Rushing blackness surrounded her and she fell.

Darkness. She was on a ship—no, she wasn't. She was fighting, struggling in icy water. Cassie clawed out, trying to get to the surface. She couldn't *see*—

"Take it easy! You're safe. Cassie, it's all right."

A wet cloth fell away from Cassie's eyes. She was in Diana's living room, lying on the couch. It was dim because the curtains were drawn and the lamps were off. Diana was leaning over her, and the long, silvery cascade of Diana's hair was falling down like a shield between Cassie and the world.

"Diana!" She clung to the other girl's hand.

"It's all right. You're okay. You're okay."

Cassie let out her breath, leaning back against the couch, her eyes meeting Diana's.

"Jack Brunswick is Black John." It was a flat statement.

"I know," Diana said grimly. "After you went down we all saw the ring. I don't think he expected us to recognize him so fast."

"What happened? What did he do?" Cassie was envisioning chaos at the cemetery.

"Not much. He left as we were carrying you to my car. Adam and Deborah went after him, but they weren't obvious about it. They're going to try to follow him. Nobody else—none of the adults—realized anything was wrong. They just figured you were exhausted. Mr. Humphries said maybe you'd better take some time off from school."

"Maybe we'd all better," Cassie whispered. Her head was spinning. Black John in charge of the school. What in the name of God was he planning?

"You said Adam went after him?" she asked, and Diana nodded. Cassie felt a pang of anxiety—and frustration. She wanted Adam *here*, so she could talk to him. She needed him. . . .

"Hey, everything okay in there?" Chris and Doug were hanging in the doorway, as if it were a lady's boudoir that they weren't allowed inside of.

"She's all right," Diana said.

"You sure, Cassie?" Chris asked, venturing a few steps in. Cassie nodded wanly, then suddenly thought of Sally's words in the bathroom. *She's the kind guys are just dying to take care of.* That certainly wasn't true . . . was it? Sally had warped everything; she'd had it all wrong.

"Come on, you two, there's double-fudge cake in the kitchen," Diana said to the brothers. "Everybody in the neighborhood's been dropping food off, and we need help eating it." Cassie thought it was strange that Diana was leaving her, then she saw that Chris and Doug hadn't been alone.

Nick was standing in the hallway outside the living room. When Diana ushered the Henderson brothers out, he came in, walking slowly.

"Uh . . . hi, Nick," Cassie said.

He gave her an odd, fleeting smile and sat on the arm of the couch. His customary mask of stone was gone today. In the dim room, Cassie thought he looked a little tired, a little sad, but maybe that was only her imagination.

"How're you doing?" he said. "You had us scared for a minute there."

Nick, scared? Cassie didn't believe it. "I'm fine, now," she said, and then she tried to think of something else to say. It was the same as it had been with Portia: when she really needed it, her mind wouldn't work.

The silence stretched out. Nick was looking at the scrolls and flowers on the upholstery of the couch. "Cassie," he said finally, "I've been meaning to talk to you."

"Oh, have you," Cassie said faintly. She felt very strange; hot and embarrassed and at the same time weak. She didn't want Nick to go on—but some part of her did.

"I realize this isn't exactly the perfect moment," he said ironically, transferring his gaze to the wallpaper. "But the way things are going we may all be dead before the perfect moment comes." Cassie opened her mouth, but no sound came out, and Nick was going on, relentlessly, inevitably, his voice low but perfectly audible. "I know you and Conant were pretty attached to each other," he said. "And I know you thought a lot of him. I realize I'm hardly the perfect substitute—but like I said, the way things are going maybe it's stupid to wait for perfection." Suddenly he was looking directly at her and Cassie saw something in his mahogany eyes she'd never seen before. "So, Cassie, what do you think about it?" Nick said. "About you and me?"

FIVE

Cassie opened her mouth to speak, but Nick was going on.

"You know, when I first saw you I thought you were just ordinary," he said. "Then I started noticing things about you—your hair, your mouth. The way you kept on fighting even when you were scared. That night when Lovejoy was killed you were scared to death, but you were the one who suggested we look for the dark energy, and when we were out at the burying ground you kept up with Deborah." Nick stopped and grinned ruefully. "And with us guys," he said.

Cassie felt an answering smile tug at her own lips; quickly suppressed it. "Nick, I . . ."

"Don't say anything yet. I want you to know that I—felt bad about how I treated you when you came to ask me to the dance." His jaw was tight, and he looked steadily at one particular flower on the upholstery of the couch. "I don't know why I did it—I've just got a lousy temper, I guess. I've had it so long I don't even think about it anymore." Nick took a deep breath before continuing, "See, I've always hated living with Deb's parents; I always felt like I *owed* them something. It put me in a permanent bad mood, I guess. I felt like my mom and dad screwed up somehow, getting themselves killed in a hurricane so their kid had to be supported by other people. It made me hate them—and my aunt and uncle, too."

Nick stopped and shook his head thoughtfully. "Yeah, especially Aunt Grace. She talks about my dad all the time, goin' on and on about how reckless he was, how he didn't care who he left behind, that kind of crap. It made me sick. I never figured it could be because she missed him."

Cassie was fascinated. "Is that why you don't like magic?" It was a blind guess, but he looked at her, startled.

"I don't know—I suppose it could have

something to do with it. I resented the rest of the coven because I felt like they all had a better deal than me. They all had at least a grandparent, and I just had my dead parents that screwed up. And they were all so damn *cheerful* about it—like Conant. He—" Nick paused and glanced up at Cassie wryly. "Well, maybe the less said about him, the better. Anyway, I know the truth now. My parents didn't screw up, and if *I* screw up I can't blame them anymore. I've got only one person to blame—me. So I'm sorry about the way I acted."

"Nick, that's okay. You did take me to the dance."

"Yeah, after you came back and asked again. That took guts. And after I took you we went to Number Thirteen and you got hurt." The corner of Nick's mouth turned down. "I couldn't do anything about that. It was Conant who saved you."

A memory of the smoky thing at the Halloween ceremony, the dark form that had risen out of the Samhain fire, flickered through Cassie's mind. She shoved it away, feeling panic rise in her chest. She didn't want to think about Black John now—frightening though he had been as a smoky figure, he was more frightening by far as a man. His eyes . . .

"Cassie." Nick's strong fingers were wrapped around her wrist. "It's okay. You're okay."

Cassie gulped a deep breath and nodded, her awareness returning to the dim room. "Thanks," she whispered. It felt good to have Nick's hand on her arm: warm fingers, firm grip. It steadied her. And, God, she'd needed somebody to hang on to, for so long . . . She remembered sitting in Adam's car, aching with the need to hold him, to be held. And knowing that she couldn't, that she never could. Cassie had that same ache now, and Adam was completely lost to her. How long did she have to live with the empty feeling?

"I know," Nick was saying in a low voice, "that you're not in love with me. I know I'm not him. But, Cassie, I like you. I like you a lot, more than any girl I've ever seen. You're so decent to people, you're not hard, but inside you're tough as Deb. Tough as me, maybe." He laughed shortly. "You haven't kept a grudge against anybody in the Club, no matter how they treated you in the beginning. Deb was really surprised about that. And in the end you've made them all respect you. The Henderson brothers never fell for a girl before, but they don't know if they're on their heads or their feet anymore. I think they're going to make you a pipe bomb for Christmas."

Cassie couldn't help laughing with him. "Well, I guess that's one way to get rid of the problem."

"Even Faye respects you," Nick said. "She wouldn't have tried so hard to destroy you otherwise. Look, Cassie, I can't explain what it is about you—you're good but you're tough. You can take it. And you've got the most gorgeous eyes I've ever seen."

Cassie felt the blood rising to her face. She could feel his eyes on her, and *she* was the one forced to study the wallpaper. The hot, strange feeling inside her was stronger every minute.

She was thinking about that first week of school, when Deborah and the Henderson brothers had been teasing her, playing keep-away with her backpack—and suddenly a brown arm had reached into her field of vision, catching the backpack, saving her. Nick. And about how nice he'd been in the boiler room when she'd found Jeffrey's body, how he'd held her and said, "Steady, steady." His arms had been solid and comforting then. Nick wasn't intimidated by anything. She liked Nick.

But liking wasn't enough.

Cassie found herself shaking her head. "Nick—I'm so sorry. I can't lead you on . . . "

"I said I knew you weren't in love with me. But if you just want to give it a try—I'll be there when you need somebody. We could have some fun," he added, as lightly as she'd ever heard Nick speak. "Get to know each other."

Cassie thought about how annoyed she'd been a while ago that Adam wasn't here at Diana's. She didn't have the right to demand Adam like that—and it was dangerous. *I'll be there when you need somebody.* How could Nick know how important that was to her?

She looked up at him, and in a voice she herself could barely hear, she said, "Okay."

The mahogany eyes widened slightly in surprise—which by Nick's normally expressionless standards translated into astonishment. A wondering smile curved his lips a little. He looked so happy that Cassie felt herself drawn into it. Why could she never resist smiling back at him?

"I didn't think you'd go for it," he said, still wonderingly.

Cassie laughed, but blushed harder. "So why did you ask?"

"I figured it was worth asking, even if you told me to get lost."

"Nick." Cassie felt something strange. "I wouldn't ever tell you to get lost. You're—well, you're really special." She didn't know how to say what she meant, and the words caught in her throat anyway. Her vision was blurring, swimming. She blinked to clear it and felt tears spill. And then Nick moved toward her and somehow she was in his arms, crying on his shoulder. Nothing had ever been so comforting as that gray-wool-clad shoulder.

She sniffled and she could feel him leaning his cheek against her hair. "Let's just give it a try for a while," he said softly. And Cassie nodded and let herself rest in his arms.

It was dark when she let Nick out the front door. Diana was upstairs; Chris and Doug had left a long time ago. Cassie felt uncertain and shy as she tapped on Diana's door.

"Come in," Diana said, and Cassie did, remembering the first time she'd tapped on this door and come into this room, the day Diana had rescued her from Faye in the science building. Then, Diana had been sitting at the window seat, surrounded by a whirling crowd of rainbows. Now Diana was sitting at the desk with a pile of papers in front of her.

"So what happened?" she said, turning around.

Cassie could feel the heat in her cheeks. "I—we—we decided that we would give it a try. Being—well, sort of being together, I mean."

Diana's lips parted. She looked into Cassie's eyes, as if searching for something there. "You *what?*" she said, and then she caught herself. She looked at Cassie for another long moment. "I see," she said slowly.

"You're not mad?" Cassie was trying to figure out what was going on behind those emerald-green eyes.

"Mad? How could I be mad at you? I'm just—surprised, that's all. But don't worry about it. Nick's a nice guy, and I know you won't hurt him. You know how special he is."

Cassie nodded, but she was startled to hear her own words on Diana's lips. She hadn't known *Diana* knew.

"No, I think it's a good thing," Diana said firmly, pushing the papers out of the way.

Cassie breathed a sigh of relief. Then she looked at the papers Diana had been examining when she came in. They were old and yellowing, covered with thick strokes of black writing in columns. The writing had some odd curlicues in it and little punctuation that Cassie could see, but it was legible.

"What are these?"

"Black John's personal papers. Letters and things—we gathered them all up when we started looking for the Master Tools. I was looking through them to see if maybe I could find some weakness that we can use against him, to fight him. That's how we found out where to look for the crystal skull in the first place; he wrote a letter about it to one of Sean's ancestors and we found it in Sean's attic. Not giving the exact location of the island, of course, but giving some clues."

"I didn't realize he would trust anybody enough to give them clues."

"He didn't. Apparently, he was planning to go back and get the skull, either to use it or to put it somewhere safer, but he died before he could do it."

"He drowned," Cassie murmured, turning over a small rectangular paper in her fingers. It was printed *Massachusetts-Bay Colony, 8 dollars*. Good grief, it was money, money from the 1600s.

"You said that before," Diana said, eyeing Cassie thoughtfully. "I wondered then how you knew."

"What? Oh, I guess one of you told me." Cassie tried to think. "Maybe Melanie."

"Melanie couldn't have told you. None of us could have, Cassie, because none of us ever knew it. You're the first person who's suggested he died at sea."

"But . . ." Bewildered, Cassie searched her mind, trying to think where she'd come up with the idea. "But then how . . ." Suddenly she knew. "My dreams," she whispered, backing up to the bed. "Oh, Diana, he's been in my dreams. I *dreamed* about drowning, about being on a ship that was going down. But it wasn't me, it was him. It was Black John."

"Cassie." Diana came over and sat down beside her. "Are you sure it was him?"

"*Yes*. Because it happened again today, when I saw him at the cemetery. I looked into his eyes—and then I felt myself falling. Drowning. There was salt water all around me, and it was cold. I could taste it."

Diana put her arms around Cassie's heaving shoulders. "Don't think about it anymore."

"I'm all right," Cassie whispered. "But why

would he make me go through that? Why would he put it in my head? Is he trying to kill me?"

"I don't know," Diana said, her voice unsteady. "Cassie, I told you before, you don't have to stay here—"

"I *do*, though." Cassie thought of her grandmother, and words echoed in her mind. *There's nothing frightening in the dark, if you just face it.*

The ocean was dark, dark as midnight underwater, and cold as hematite. But I can face that, Cassie thought. I refuse to be afraid of it. I refuse. She pushed the fear away from her and slowly felt the trembling inside her steady.

My line has the sight and the power, she thought. I want to use that power to stand up to him. To face him.

She drew away from Diana. "I think you've got the right idea tonight," she said, nodding at the papers on the desk. "You go through those, and your Book of Shadows, and I'll keep going through mine." She looked at the window seat where the red leather-covered book lay beside a block of multicolored Post-it notes and a scattering of felt-tip pens and highlighters.

"Have you found anything interesting so far?" Diana asked as Cassie settled into the window seat with the book on her lap.

"Nothing about Black John. In the beginning the spells seem to be pretty much the same as yours. But everything in it's interesting, and who knows what's going to turn out to be useful in the end," Cassie said. She was determined to get familiar with the range of spells and amulets in the book, to learn as many as possible of them and to at least know where to find the rest. Still, it was a project that would take years, and they didn't have years. "Diana, I think we'd better talk to the old ladies in town—soon. Before—well, before anything happens so we *can't* talk to them." She met Diana's eyes grimly.

Diana blinked, taking in Cassie's meaning, and then nodded. "You're right. He's already killed four people, at least. If he thinks they're a threat . . ." She swallowed. "We'll talk to them tomorrow. I'll tell Adam when he calls—he's supposed to call me when he and Deborah get through shadowing Black John."

"I hope Black John doesn't know he's being shadowed," Cassie said.

"I hope so too," Diana said quietly, and bent her head over the papers again.

* * *

The meeting was held the next day on the beach. Faye didn't have a chance to veto the location because Faye wasn't there.

"She's with *him*," Deborah said briefly. "I followed her this morning—Adam and I flipped for it last night. She met him at that same coffee shop where they met yesterday—"

"Hang on, hang on," Laurel said. "You're getting ahead of yourself. What coffee shop?"

"I'll tell it," Adam said, in response to Diana's look. "Yesterday we went out of the cemetery and followed—Mr. Brunswick. That's a joke, by the way."

Diana nodded. "I used to do a little oil-painting, and Brunswick is a kind of paint," she told Cassie and the group. "Black paint."

"Very funny," said Cassie. She was sitting beside Nick, a new position, and one that made her slightly self-conscious. She was very aware of him, of his arm beside her. If she leaned a little to the right, she could touch him, and it was comforting. "I wonder what he did with the real person who was supposed to be principal," she said.

"I don't know." Adam couldn't have helped but notice who she was sitting by, and the new expression in Nick's eyes, a sort of

85

protectiveness. Right now Cassie could see his blue-gray gaze flicker toward Nick, looking him up and down narrowly. It wasn't a friendly look. "I don't know how he managed to get the position. I don't know *why* he would want it, either." He glanced at Nick again and opened his mouth, but Diana was talking.

"Go on with the story. Go on, Adam. Tell us what happened when you followed him yesterday."

"Huh? Oh, right. Well, he left alone, in a gray Cadillac, and we followed; Deborah on her bike and me in my jeep. He drove into town and went to the Perko's Koffee Kup there—and guess who drove up a few minutes later?"

"Wearing a black lace minidress and looking *really* perky," Deborah put in.

"Faye," Diana whispered, looking sick. "How *could* she?"

"I dunno, but she did," Deborah said. "We watched her through the window, and she went to his booth. He's a living, breathing man, all right—he was drinking coffee. They talked for about an hour. Faye was prancing and tossing her head like a little filly in a show. And he seemed to like it—anyway, he was smiling at her."

"We waited until they left, then Deb followed her and I followed him," Adam said. "He drove to a summer cottage on the mainland—I guess he's rented it. He stayed there all night, I think; I finally left around one in the morning."

"Where did Faye go?" Melanie asked Deborah.

Deborah made a face. "I don't know."

"Why not?"

"Because she lost me, okay? Riding a Harley isn't exactly inconspicuous. She started going through red lights and suddenly making U-turns, and in the end she lost me. You want to make something out of it?"

"Deb," Cassie said. Deborah scowled at her, then rolled her eyes and shrugged.

"Anyway, this morning I waited outside her house, and she went back to meet him. They had a booth at the back, though, not near a window. So I went inside, but I really couldn't see what was going on. I *think* she gave him something, but I don't know what."

"Wonderful," Suzan said, and Deborah glared at her.

"I mean, wonderful that she's—what do you call it? In league with him. Is anybody going to eat that doughnut?" Suzan daintily shook off powdered sugar and bit in.

Laurel murmured something about white sugar being worse than rat poison, but she didn't have the energy to say more.

"It's *good*," Suzan said indistinctly. "The only thing it's missing is cream filling."

"I think we'd better go talk with the old ladies," Cassie said. "With Adam's grandmother, I mean, and Laurel's grandmother and Melanie's great-aunt."

"Today's a good day," Melanie volunteered. "Every Sunday afternoon they get together and have lunch at our place: a kind of tea, you know, with sandwiches and little cakes and stuff."

"That's right," Cassie said. "My grandmother used to go too."

"Cakes?" said Suzan, looking interested. "Why didn't you say so? Let's go."

"Right—no, wait," Diana said. She looked around the group. "Look, it's probably pointless to ask this, but did any of *you* take the piece of hematite out of Cassie's room?" Everyone stared at her, then at each other. Everyone except Cassie and Laurel. Heads were shaken, and all the faces wore the same look of puzzlement.

"Somebody took the hematite?" Deborah

asked. "The piece you found at Number Thirteen?" Cassie nodded, unobtrusively studying the other members of the Circle. Adam was frowning, the Henderson brothers looked blank. Sean looked nervous, but then Sean always looked nervous. Melanie seemed troubled, Nick was slowly shaking his head, and Suzan was shrugging.

"I didn't think anybody would admit to it," Diana said. "But I suspect that's because the person who took it isn't here. She's at Perko's Koffee Kup." Diana sighed. "All right. Let's go to Number Four."

Cassie had been getting quite familiar with Melanie's house since her mother had been taken to stay there. The house was in the Federal style, very similar to Cassie's grandmother's, but in much better repair. The white clapboard walls were freshly painted and everything inside had a shipshape, tidy look. Great-aunt Constance was sitting in the front parlor with old Mrs. Franklin, Adam's grandmother, and Laurel's Granny Quincey. She didn't look at all pleased to see the eleven of them crowding in the parlor door.

"Great-aunt Constance? Can we talk to you?"
The elderly woman turned a cool,

disapproving eye on Melanie. She was thin and regal, and in her high-cheekboned face Cassie could detect some resemblance to Melanie's classic beauty. Her hair was still very dark, but maybe she dyed it.

"Are you here to see your mother?" she said, spotting Cassie in the group. "She's fast asleep right now; I really don't think she should be disturbed."

"Actually, Aunt Constance, we came to talk to you," Melanie said. She looked at the other women in the parlor. "To all three of you."

A line appeared between Great-aunt Constance's eyebrows, but the short plump woman sitting on the sofa said, "Oh, let them in, Connie. Why not? There you are, Adam. What kept you out so late last night, hm?"

"I didn't realize you noticed, Grandma," Adam said.

"Oh, I notice more than people think," Mrs. Franklin chuckled, picking up a cookie and popping it into her mouth. Her gray hair was piled untidily on her head in braids, and there was a disorganized air about her that contrasted with the austere white and gold parlor. Cassie liked her.

"What's going on, Laurel?" a quavery voice

asked, and Cassie looked at Granny Quincey, a tiny woman with a face like a dried apple. She was actually Laurel's great-grandmother, and she was so little and light she looked as if a puff of wind would blow her away.

"Well—" Laurel looked at Adam, who spoke up.

"Actually, it has something to do with what my grandmother asked me. What I was out doing last night. And it has to do with something that happened a long time ago, right around the time all of us kids were born."

Great-aunt Constance was really frowning now, and Granny Quincey's lips were pursed together. Old Mrs. Franklin was chuckling, but she was looking around the room in a way that made Cassie wonder if she'd really heard her grandson.

"Well?" Great-aunt Constance said sharply. "Explain yourself."

Adam glanced back at the rest of the Circle, all of whom were beaconing their support, silently electing him spokesman. He took a deep breath and turned back to the old women.

"What I was out doing was shadowing our new high-school principal, Mr. Jack Brunswick," he said. The name elicited no reaction. "I think you might have known him under a different name." Utter silence.

"The name we're all most familiar with is Black John," said Adam.

The silence was shattered as Great-aunt Constance stood so abruptly that one of the fragile willow-patterned tea cups dashed to the floor.

"Get out of this house! Get out!" she said to Adam.

SIX

"Aunt Constance!" Melanie gasped.

"You heard me," the dark-haired woman said to Adam. She looked at the rest of the group. "Get out of here, all of you! I don't like that kind of joke, especially now. Haven't you made enough trouble with your meddling? Poor Alexandra in the guest room, and Maeve scarcely in the ground . . . Melanie, I want them out of the house!"

Laurel and Granny Quincey were both fluttering. "Oh dear, oh dear," Granny Quincey was saying, raising hands that looked like little bird claws, and "Oh, please, Miss Burke," Laurel was beseeching, almost in tears.

"You have no respect at all," Aunt Constance

said, breathing hard. Her eyes were as bright as if she had a fever.

"Young people never do, Constance," Adam's grandmother said, chuckling. "Why, I remember when we were their age, the mischief we used to get up to . . . oh, me." Still laughing and shaking her head, Adam's grandmother popped another cookie in her mouth.

"Grandma, please listen. It's not a joke," Adam began helplessly, but it was no use. There was too much noise; everyone was talking at once. Over it all Great-aunt Constance continued to order them out, telling Melanie to forget about the mess on the floor and just *go*. Granny Quincey was twittering and making calming gestures, which everybody ignored. Old Mrs. Franklin was smiling at them all benevolently. Diana was pleading with Melanie's aunt to listen, but to no avail.

"For the last time!" Aunt Constance cried, flapping a hand as if to shoo Diana and the Club out the door.

"Miss Burke!" Cassie yelled. She felt close to tears herself, although Nick had been quietly trying to escort her out since the shouting had started. Cassie didn't want to go; she thought she understood what Great-aunt Constance was talking about when she mentioned the kids' meddling. "Miss Burke," she repeated, forcing her way forward again. She found herself directly in front of Great-aunt Constance.

"I'm sorry," Cassie said, and it was suddenly quiet enough that she could hear the unsteadiness in her own voice. "It's my mom that's in your guest room, and you know how grateful I am that you're taking care of her. And it's my grandmother that's in the ground. But who do you think did that to them? It wasn't the Club. My grandmother told me before she died that he had planned all along to come back, and that she always knew he would manage to do it. It's true that it's partly the Circle's fault he's back—it's partly *my* fault. And we're sorry, more sorry than you can know. But he really is here." She paused a moment, then added in almost a whisper, "Really."

Aunt Constance was breathing very quickly through her nose. She drew herself up more regally than ever, her lips a thin red slash across her face.

"I'm afraid I can't believe any of what you're saying. It is simply im–impossible—" The woman's expression changed, twisting in pain. She gave a gasp and clutched at her chest.

"Aunt Constance," Melanie cried, rushing to her. It took both her and Adam to help the rigid woman to a chair.

"Should I call a doctor?" Diana asked.

"No!" Aunt Constance said, lifting her head. "It's nothing. I'm all right now."

"It's not nothing, Constance," a quavery voice said, and Cassie saw Granny Quincey getting off the sofa to come stand beside the chair. "It's your heart telling you the truth. I think we'd better listen to these children."

There was a silence while Melanie's aunt looked at Melanie, then at Adam, then at Cassie. Cassie forced herself to return the piercing gaze.

Aunt Constance's eyes shut and she slowly leaned back in the chair.

"You're right," she said, without looking at anyone. "Come in, all of you, and find somewhere to sit down. Then you can tell your story."

"So finally we decided we'd better talk to you three, since you were the ones who might remember him from the last time," Diana said. "We thought of asking our parents, too—"

"Don't go to your parents," Aunt Constance

96

said flatly. She had sat and listened to the whole tale, her expression getting grimmer and grimmer. An aura of bleak horror hung in the room. "They wouldn't understand," she said, and her gaze settled on Cassie emptily, making Cassie think of her mother's blank eyes. "They won't remember. Dear God, how I've wished that *I* could forget too . . ."

"What's past is past," Granny Quincey said.

"Yes," said Great-aunt Constance. She straightened. "But I don't know how you think three old women are going to help you—against *him.*"

"We thought that you might remember something about him, some weakness; something we can use to fight him," Adam said.

Aunt Constance slowly shook her head. Granny Quincey was frowning, her face pursed into hundreds of wrinkles. Old Mrs. Franklin wore a very pleasant expression; Cassie couldn't tell if she'd been following the story or not.

"If he can come back from the dead, he can't have many weaknesses," Aunt Constance whispered harshly. "And he was always clever at manipulating. You say that Faye Chamberlain is on his side?"

"We're afraid so," Adam said.

"That's bad. He'll use her to get at you, at *your* weaknesses. Lure her away from him if you can. But how?" Aunt Constance's brow lined in concentration. "The hematite—take that from her. It's very dangerous; he can use it to influence her mind." Diana glanced at Cassie, as if to say, *I told you.* Aunt Constance was going on. "And you say the skull is gone now? Are you sure?"

"It's gone," Adam said.

"It looked like it exploded when Faye was holding it, just before we were all knocked out," Cassie said. "Something exploded *out* of it, anyway. And we couldn't find a trace of it afterward."

"Well . . . there's no way to use that against him, then. And you, Cassie, you haven't found anything in your grandmother's Book to help you?"

"Not yet. I haven't gotten all the way through it, though," Cassie admitted.

Aunt Constance was shaking her head. "Power, you need power to use against him. You're all too young to fight him—and we're too old. And in between our ages are nothing but fools. There's no power strong enough around here . . ."

"There was once," Granny Quincey said in her reedy voice.

Aunt Constance looked at her, and her expression changed. "Once . . . yes, of course." She turned to the Circle. "If the old stories are true, there once was a power strong enough to destroy Black John."

"What power?" Laurel asked.

Aunt Constance countered with a question. "How did Adam happen to find the skull, exactly?"

"It wasn't an accident," Diana said. "He was out looking for the Master Tools . . ." She stopped. "The Master Tools," she whispered.

"Yes. The ones that belonged to the original coven, the real Salem witches. Our ancestors who founded New Salem after the witch hunters drove them out of Salem Village."

Cassie was speaking out loud before she thought. "But just what *were* the Master Tools, exactly?"

It was Granny Quincey who answered. "The symbols of the witch leader, of course. The diadem, the bracelet, and the garter."

"The ones we use are just imitations," Melanie said. "They *are* just symbols. The original coven's were very powerful; real tools to be used.

But, Aunt Constance"—she turned back to her aunt—"it was Black John who hid the Master Tools. Adam's been looking for them for years, from here to Cape Cod. How can we find them now?"

"I don't know," the woman said. "But you've got one thing wrong there. Black John didn't hide them, the original coven did. They hid the tools *from* him, so he wouldn't be able to use them. They knew that with the power of the skull and the tools together, he would be invincible. That's what *my* grandmother told me, anyway."

"They wouldn't have taken the tools far to hide," Granny Quincey added. "That's just sense. Black John was a traveler, but our ancestors weren't. They were peaceable, home-loving people."

"You came for our advice—well, that's mine," Aunt Constance said. "Find the Master Tools. If you all stand together, using those, you may have a chance against him." Her lips were a thin line again.

"All right," Adam said slowly. "We understand."

Cassie let her breath out, trying not to feel disappointed. It was good advice, but she'd hoped—for what? For her own grandmother, she supposed. She wanted her grandmother, who had been so wise, and had somehow always made Cassie feel as if she were stronger than she'd thought.

"And keep reading that book your grandma gave you!" Granny Quincey said suddenly, looking right at Cassie. Cassie nodded and the old woman gave her a wrinkled but oddly intense smile.

Mrs. Franklin was smiling too, patting her knees and looking around as if she'd forgotten something.

"What's tomorrow?" she said.

There was a pause. Cassie wasn't sure if Adam's grandmother was speaking to them or to herself. But then she repeated, "What's tomorrow?" looking at them encouragingly.

"Uh—our birthday," Chris offered.

But Diana looked startled. "I think—I think it's the night of Hecate," she said. "Is that what you mean?"

"That's right," old Mrs. Franklin said comfortably. "Oh, when I was young, we would have done a ceremony. I remember ceremonies under the moon, when there were Indians in the shadows . . ."

Glances were exchanged. Mrs. Franklin couldn't possibly remember that; there hadn't been Indians around here for centuries.

But Diana was getting excited. "You think we should have a ceremony?"

"*I* would, dear," Mrs. Franklin said. "A girls' ceremony. We girls always had our secrets, didn't we, Connie? And we stuck together."

Diana looked a little puzzled, then nodded slowly, determinedly. "Yes. *Yes.* It would be good for the girls to get together—*all* the girls. And I think I know what kind of ceremony to have. It's not the right time of year, but that doesn't matter."

"I know you'll enjoy it, dear," Mrs. Franklin said. "Now let me see—Cassie!"

Cassie looked at her, startled.

"Cassie," Adam's grandmother said again. Her head was on one side, and she was sighing, the way you do when somebody shows you a picture of smiling baby. "Dear me, you are a pretty little thing, though you don't look at all like your mother. Still—" She broke off suddenly and looked around. "Hm?"

Great-aunt Constance was looking more severe than ever, her snapping eyes right on Mrs. Franklin. "Edith," she said, in a flat voice.

Mrs. Franklin looked at Granny Quincey, who was also staring at her with great concentration.

"Why—I was only going to say I could see a bit of her mother in her expression," she said, and nodded at Cassie pleasantly. "You try not to worry so much, dear. It'll all come right in the end."

Aunt Constance relaxed almost imperceptibly. "Yes. That's all, Melanie; you'd better take your friends away."

And that was that. The eleven of them got up and said thank you and good-bye politely, and then they were outside the big white house in the thin November sunlight.

"Whew!" said Cassie. "Adam, do you know what was going on there at the end?"

"Sorry," Adam said, grimacing. "She gets like that sometimes."

"It wasn't her so much as the other two," Cassie began, but Deborah broke in, impatient.

"So what's this night of Hecate thing?"

"It's the night of the crone," Diana said. "That's what Hecate stands for."

"The crone?" Suzan echoed in distaste, and Cassie knew what she meant. The word conjured up an unpleasant image—a stooped, wrinkled figure holding up a poisoned apple.

"Yes." Diana looked at Cassie. "It's not a bad thing, Cassie. Crone just means old woman—it's the last stage in a woman's life. Maiden, mother, then crone. Crones are wise and—well, tough. Not physically, maybe, but mentally. They've seen a lot; they've been through it, and they know things. They're the ones who pass things on to us."

"Like my grandmother," Cassie said, understanding dawning. Of course—that stooped, wrinkled figure was the very picture of her grandmother. Not a poisoned apple, then, she thought. If her grandmother offered anything to anybody, it was help. "Fairy tales give us the wrong idea," she said.

"Right." Diana nodded firmly. "When I'm old I hope I'm a crone like your grandmother."

"Whatever you want," Doug said, rolling his eyes.

"They're all trying to help," Melanie said. "Even Aunt Constance. But what are we going to do for the night of Hecate, Diana?"

"It's a night for fortune-telling and prophecies," Diana said, "and we have to find a crossroads where we can celebrate it. Hecate was the Greek goddess of crossroads—they're supposed to symbolize transformation. Starting on a new passage of life. It could be old age, or death, or some other kind of change."

"I think we're all at a crossroads," Melanie said soberly.

"I do too." Diana looked at Adam. "I think your grandmother was right; this is something we girls should do. But that'll leave you guys alone . . ."

Adam grinned. "Oh, I guess we could manage to amuse ourselves for one night without you. Maybe Chris and Doug have some ideas." He spoke easily; Cassie had noticed that all the guys in the Circle were undisturbed by the girls' rights and privileges. They didn't feel threatened; they seemed to know that they were just as important, in a different way.

"But I think you should be very careful," Nick said, without a trace of humor in his voice. Chris and Doug were punching each other, arguing about how they wanted to celebrate their birthday. When Nick spoke they shut up.

"I think you'd better find a crossroads right near here," Nick went on, speaking to Diana and Cassie. "And that we'd better not be too far away."

Cassie looked into his face, saw the concern behind the careful control in his eyes. She took his hand, felt his strong fingers interlace with hers.

"We'll be careful," she promised quietly. She saw Deborah's sharp glance at their linked hands, saw a knowing grin flash across the biker girl's face. Chris was poking Doug, who was glowering indignantly. Melanie's normally cool gray eyes were wide, and Laurel and Suzan were smiling.

Cassie couldn't help but notice that Adam was *not* smiling. He didn't smile again the rest of the day.

That night, Cassie had dreams. Swirling, formless dreams that seemed to have something to do with Books of Shadows. She and Diana had been up late, reading and studying. They hadn't found anything helpful. But in Cassie's dreams she felt she was on the verge of a momentous discovery.

She caught a glimpse of the sunlit room again. Just a swift bright flash that melted almost instantly into darkness. She found herself awake, staring around Diana's bedroom as if she might find it here.

"Cassie," Diana murmured. "You okay?"

"Yes," Cassie whispered. She was glad when

Diana went still again. Diana was the one who'd insisted Cassie sleep with her, worried about Cassie having nightmares. But if Cassie really started disturbing Diana she couldn't let herself stay here anymore. She was enough trouble to Diana without keeping her up all night.

Actually, Cassie had slept very peacefully in the Meade house. It wasn't like Number Twelve, which had groaned and popped so much in settling that Cassie had been constantly jolted awake. Some difference in the way the houses were made, she supposed. The additions to Diana's house were much newer; perhaps they'd used better materials.

Cassie lay for a while in the warm darkness, listening to Diana's soft breathing. Where was Black John tonight? she wondered. Out there on the mainland in his rented cottage? Or here, on the island of New Salem?

For some reason thinking of New Salem as an island upset her. She felt—isolated, somehow: besieged. As if Black John could cut all of them off from the rest of the world and cast them adrift on the ocean.

Don't be silly, she told herself. But the threads of panic churning in her stomach wouldn't be stilled. She wondered suddenly if her mother wouldn't be better off in an institution—away from here. Anywhere away from here.

There's no reason for him to hurt her. It's us he hates, she thought desperately.

But he had come after her grandmother. Why? For the Book of Shadows?

I'm the one who has the Book of Shadows now, she realized with a sick lurch of heart. What if he decides to come and take it?

The thought grabbed hold of her imagination. She could feel the bed quiver with the pounding of her heart. What if Black John were to come here, now? He was a living, breathing man—but he was also a witch. Was he bound by the rules of other men? Or could he come sliding in here like a shadow, crawling along the floor toward the bed?

I have to stay calm. I have to. If I crack up, it's all over. For Mom, for the coven, for everyone. It's going to take all of us to fight him. I can't be the weak link.

"There is nothing frightening in the dark if you just face it," she whispered to herself between clenched teeth. "There is nothing frightening in the dark if you just face it."

Burning tears spilled out of her eyes, but she kept on whispering her grandmother's phrase.

On and on until at last she fell asleep.

The next school day began with an assembly. Faye hadn't been in her normal seat in writing class again, but as Cassie filed into the auditorium she was astonished to see the dark-haired girl up by the stage.

Faye was standing quietly, almost demurely—for Faye. She was wearing a tailored suit and looked like a very smart, very sexy secretary. Her mane of dark hair was piled up softly on her head, and she was carrying a stack of papers and a clipboard. All she needed was a pair of horn-rimmed glasses and she could have been some billionaire's girl Friday.

Cassie couldn't believe it.

She looked around the auditorium and caught sight of Suzan and Sean, who both had the same remedial-English class first period. She jerked her chin at them and they split off from their class and joined her. Suzan's blue eyes were enormous.

"Did you see Faye? What's she doing up there?"

"I don't know," Cassie said. "Nothing good."

"She *looks* good," Sean said, wetting his lips quickly. "She looks great."

Cassie glanced at Sean, really noticing him for the first time in a long time. Since she'd danced with him at the Halloween dance, maybe. It was so easy to overlook Sean; in a crowd he just seemed to blend in. But here, with only him and Suzan beside her, Cassie focused.

I should pay more attention to him, she thought. An image skittered through her mind: Sean as he had appeared the first time she'd seen him. Shiny eyes, shiny belt engraved with his name. Standing by his locker full of Soloflex ads, grinning at her. Something about the picture disturbed her profoundly, but she couldn't think what.

The last of the junior and senior classes were coming into the auditorium. Cassie saw the Henderson brothers and Deborah sitting down with their history class. There was Diana and Melanie and Laurel from British Literature, and Sally Waltman, too, with the now-familiar straw-colored head of Portia Bainbridge next to her. She saw Adam and his chemistry class, but didn't spot Nick.

"Looks like Faye's doing a little extracurricular activity," a voice behind her murmured, and Cassie turned gratefully. Nick nodded at the guy who was occupying the seat there, and the guy scrambled up and left. Cassie hardly noticed the occurrence, it was so common. The kids from Crowhaven Road indicated what they wanted, and the outsiders gave it to them. Always. It was the way things worked.

Nick sat in the vacated chair and took out a pack of cigarettes. He opened it, shook one forward. Then he noticed Cassie.

Cassie was staring at him with her eyebrows lifted, her best Diana expression on. Disapproval radiating from her like heat waves.

"Ah," Nick said. He glanced at the cigarettes, then at her again. He tapped the protruding cigarette back into place and tucked the pack in his pocket.

"Bad habit," he said.

"Testing, one, two, three . . ." It was Faye's voice over the microphone. Cassie turned quickly.

"It's on," Faye said, with a smile Cassie could only describe as kittenish. Faye moved away from the lectern, and the tall man also standing onstage walked up to it. He adjusted it, his eyes on the crowd of seated students.

"Good morning," he said, and his voice sent waves of darkness crashing through Cassie. Every muscle in her body tightened defensively, ready to obey some deeply buried instinct to fight or flee. Just his voice, she thought dazedly, how can someone's voice alone do that?

"As some of you already know, I'm Mr. Brunswick, your new principal."

SEVEN

There was a scattering of applause, hesitant, dying away quickly. Already the atmosphere in the auditorium was uncertain, alert. The usual whispers and fidgets snuffed out like candle flames, until the great room was utterly still. All eyes were on the stage.

He's a handsome man, Cassie thought, fighting the pounding in her brain that was telling her to run, run. Why did she react so violently to his presence? It was like her reaction on the night of her initiation, when Adam had produced the crystal skull. Cassie had taken one look at it and felt horror creep up her spine—to her, it seemed surrounded by a halo of darkness. It had only been later that she realized not all the coven members could see what she saw.

As Cassie looked around now, she could tell by the expressions of the other students that they didn't feel the darkness emanating from the new principal. To her, he cast a shadow across the entire auditorium. To them, he simply seemed powerful, impressive.

"I realize there has been some turmoil at New Salem High School recently," he was saying, his eyes moving slowly up and down the rows of students. Cassie got the odd impression that he was memorizing each one of them. "But you'll be happy to know that's over now. The—unfortunate occurrences—that have plagued this school are behind us. It's time for a brand-new start."

"Turmoil" meaning two students and one principal dead, Cassie thought. Since *you* killed all three of them, I guess you can decide when it's over. At the same time she wondered exactly how he'd managed the murders from his grave. Did the dark energy itself do it? she wondered. She wanted to whisper the question to Nick or Suzan—or Sean, her mind added hastily, guiltily—but it was hard to turn her head away from the man on the stage.

"I've heard reports that the last administration's attitude toward discipline was somewhat—lenient. A policy of, shall we say, *permissiveness* which was undoubtedly intended to be benign." The principal glanced toward the teachers lining the auditorium walls, as if to intimate that he knew they might use other words to describe that policy, but there was no point in speaking ill of the dead. "Certain activities were allowed which were detrimental not only to the students they affected, but also to the very spirit of formal education. Certain groups were afforded special privileges."

What is he talking about? Cassie thought. It's like a politician; lots of fancy words and no meaning. But something inside her was sinking in dismay.

"Well, the policy has changed now, and I think in the end most of you will be pleased with the changes. There's a new hand on the tiller of this boat." The principal held up one hand with a slight, self-deprecating smile.

Then he started talking again. Afterward, Cassie could never remember exactly what he said, but she remembered his voice, deep, authoritative. Commanding. There were buzzwords scattered through his speech: "tough love," "old-fashioned discipline," "punishment fitting the crime." She could feel the response from the audience: dark, dark. Like something swelling and growing in the crowd. It frightened her almost more than Black John himself. It was as if he were feeding and cultivating some horrible power inside the students. They should have hated him, but instead they were enthralled.

The rules. The rules must be obeyed. Students who didn't obey the rules would be *sent to the office* . . .

"I think it's time for the handout now," Jack Brunswick added in a soft aside, and Faye and several other girls moved down from the stage, passing out papers. Cassie watched the principal as he watched the audience, standing at ease, commanding their attention effortlessly even when he wasn't speaking. Yes, handsome, she thought. He looked something like a young Sherlock Holmes: deep-set eyes, hawk nose, firm mouth. His voice even had traces of an English accent. Cultured, thought Cassie. Cultured—and full of conviction.

More like a witch hunter than a witch.

Faye reached Cassie's row, thrust a sheaf of papers at her. Cassie whispered "Faye!" and was rewarded by a swift flash of golden eyes before Faye moved on. Bewildered, Cassie took one handout and passed the rest to Suzan. It was three pages long and covered with small type.

Prohibited Actions—Type A. Prohibited Actions—Type B. Prohibited Actions—Type C.

It was a list of rules. But so many rules, line after line after line. Her eyes caught words here and there.

Wearing clothing inconsistent with the serious and dignified purpose of formal education . . . using a locker or being in the corridors at any time other than the passing period between classes . . . possession or use of squirt guns . . . littering . . . running in the halls . . . chewing gum . . . failing to comply with an order from any teacher or hall monitor . . .

Hall monitors? Cassie thought. We don't have hall monitors. Her eyes skimmed on.

Public displays of affection . . . failing to recycle styrofoam lunch trays . . . placing feet on seats or chair backs . . .

"They can't be serious," Suzan whispered. There was a faint whistle from Nick.

"You'll have time in class to go over these guidelines and become thoroughly familiar with them," the new principal said. In the corner of Cassie's eye she saw rows of heads lifting. The rustling of paper stilled.

"Right now I'd like to ask for volunteers to be hall monitors. This is a position of great responsibility, so please think carefully before you raise your hand."

Hands flew up all over the auditorium. The students at New Salem High had never volunteered so fast for anything. Cassie saw Portia, rigid and trembling like a hound dog pointing in the air. Sally, in the next seat, was waving madly, like a third-grader dying to get called on by the teacher. The room was like one giant Nazi salute.

Black John's eyes moved up and down, scanning them, examining each one.

Then Cassie realized that Sean's hand was going up.

"Sean!" she hissed. The auditorium was so quiet she didn't dare speak loudly. Suzan glanced at Sean, then shrank back from him. He was out of Nick's reach. "Sean!" she said.

He didn't seem to hear her. His shiny eyes were fixed on the stage. His face was eager, tense.

Desperation tingled in the palms of Cassie's

hands. She reached across Suzan to grab his left arm, and with all the power she could summon up, thought: *Sean!*

She felt it go out of her like a blast of heat, just as she'd felt it when she was facing the pumpkin-patch dog. A burst of pure power. Sean's head snapped toward her, his expression full of astonishment.

"Put your hand down," she whispered, feeling shaky and exhausted in the aftermath. Sean looked at his hand as if he'd never seen it before and hastily snatched it down. He gripped the seat of his chair, eyes still sideways on Cassie.

Now Suzan was cringing away from *her*, Cassie realized. Both the strawberry-blond and Sean looked scared. Cassie looked toward the stage and saw the new principal looking directly at her, his lips curved in a faint smile.

Great. *He* likes it, and my own friends are afraid of me.

Black John continued to gaze at her steadily for a moment, then turned the slight smile on the rest of the auditorium.

"Very good. Those of you who've been chosen will please remain after the assembly to learn about your new duties. The rest are dismissed. Good morning."

Hairs lifted on the back of Cassie's neck. "Chosen?" she whispered, looking around. There hadn't been any selection. But some of the students who'd had hands up were moving to the stage in a quiet, orderly manner. Portia and Sally were among them.

Don't you see? You've got to see now how strange this is, Cassie thought, twisting to look at Mr. Humphries standing in the aisle. But Mr. Humphries didn't seem to find anything unusual about the proceedings. He looked calm and rather pleased as he motioned his class out. *Tranquilized*, Cassie thought, shivering. Hypnotized.

Black John was still standing at the lectern. She could feel his eyes on her back as she walked out of the auditorium.

Cassie fell back as her writing class walked down the hall, slowing to stay with Nick and Suzan and Sean. Suzan and Sean looked at her oddly, but Nick put his arm around her.

"That was pretty good," he said softly. Cassie felt better, until she noticed he didn't have his handout.

"I left it on the seat," he said, and Cassie's heart sank a little further.

"That's littering," she said. "And littering's a Type-A offense. Nick, we've got to be careful—he's out to get us."

"No kidding," Adam said, joining them. His blue-gray eyes flickered once over Nick's arm around Cassie's shoulders, but his expression didn't change. "Have you read over the Prohibited Actions, Type C?"

Cassie hadn't. She thumbed to the last page of the handout and looked. "Skateboarding, roller-skating, or bike riding . . . playing or wearing radios on school grounds . . . smoking or using tobacco products . . . these are supposed to be worse than Type-B offenses like using drugs or fighting?"

"They seem to be a little specifically directed," Adam said grimly.

And then Cassie knew. She remembered her very first day of school at New Salem High, nearly being knocked off her feet by the Henderson brothers—only at the time she didn't know it was the Henderson brothers. She'd only seen two crazy guys with heavy-metal T-shirts and disheveled blond hair, rollerblading down the halls and listening to Walkmans.

She swallowed hard. "They're for *us*," she

whispered. Adam met her eyes, nodding.

"Smoking," Cassie said. She clutched Nick's hand, turning to look him full in the face. "Nick, please, you've got to be careful. He wants to get us and we're not ready to confront him yet . . . Nick!" She had a terrible feeling about this. Nick hated authority, took any rules as a challenge. Right now she didn't see any sign of him changing, by his expression. "Nick!"

"Punishment for Type-C offenses is getting sent to the office," Adam said. "He *is* trying to get us, Nick. He's playing his own little game."

"Nick, I want you to promise me you'll try not to get in trouble," Cassie said. "Please, Nick. You have to promise."

Nick looked down at her slowly. Cassie tightened her grip on his hand, returning the intensity of his gaze. Please, she was thinking. For me, please.

Nick's brow furrowed and he turned away.

"Okay," he said, nodding slightly, eyes on the ceiling. "Okay, I'll try—not to get caught."

Cassie's muscles relaxed. "Thank you," she whispered, just as Diana, Melanie, and Laurel came up, faces bleak.

"Did you get that stuff in the beginning,

about the previous administration allowing certain activities to go on?" Melanie asked. "That was *us* he was talking about. The Club and its special privileges. He said all that was going to change now."

Cassie spoke softly. "He was telling them we're not in power anymore. He was as good as giving them permission to . . ."

Her voice died away. She and the other members of the Club looked at one another silently.

"Everybody get your guns. Sounds like it's open season for witches," Nick said finally. He put his arm around Cassie again.

"Let's get out of here," Suzan said.

"We can't," said Laurel. "Leaving school grounds without permission is an offense."

"*Everything* is an offense," Suzan said.

"Where are Chris and Doug?" Cassie asked sharply. "And Deborah?"

Everyone looked around. Aside from Nick, the Henderson brothers and the biker were the ones most likely to get into trouble.

"They have history first period, but I think their class went back without them," Sean volunteered. "I think they're still in the auditorium."

"Come on," said Adam briefly.

Chris and Doug were just outside the auditorium. They were in the center of a group of outsider students and they were getting ready to fight.

"—not gonna get away with it anymore," one of the outsider boys was caroling triumphantly.

"Oh, yeah?" Chris yelled back.

"Yeah! Your days are over, man! You're gonna get *sent to the office*."

"Didn't take them long to catch on," Nick murmured in Cassie's ear.

"You're all going to get sent to the office," Adam said, pushing between the outsiders to get to Chris and Doug. He faced them, holding up the handout like a magic talisman. "Fighting's a Type-B offense. You'll *all* go down for it."

There was a moment of uncertainty, then the outsiders drew back, eyeing each other.

"We'll see you later," they decided finally, and turned down the hall. Doug tried to go after them.

"Any time, any place," he yelled as Nick caught him and held him still. "Leggo of me!" he snarled at Nick.

"We can't afford a confrontation yet," Diana

told him. "Good job," she added to Adam.

"It worked—this time," Adam said. "If I'm right about what he's doing, they'll eventually figure out that the rules are mainly against *us*. They may not get in trouble for fighting, but we will."

To Cassie's vast relief Deborah came around the corner at that moment. "Deb, where have you been?"

"Watching the hall monitors get their orders. They're giving them badges like SS men."

"It *is* like the Nazis," Cassie said.

"He's organizing a witch hunt," said Adam.

"I wonder if he's done it before," Suzan said.

Cassie started to say, "What do you mean?" but stopped in the middle of it and stared at her. Suzan, who looked so—fluffy, so brainless, who even now was groping in her purse for a compact, had done it again.

"And Faye is working for him—" Diana was saying. Cassie interrupted.

"No, wait, listen. Did you hear what Suzan just said? Don't you get it? *I wonder if he's done it before.* You know, I'll bet he has."

"In 1692," Adam said slowly. "In Salem. How could we be so stupid?"

"Huh?" said Chris.

"I think they're saying that Black John could have organized the Salem witch hunt," Diana said. "But—"

"Not organized, maybe, but contributed, helped it along," Cassie said. "Made sure it didn't just die out, fed the hysteria. Like he was feeding it today."

"But *why*?" asked Laurel.

There was a silence, then Adam lifted his head, his frown clearing. His voice was grim. "To get the coven to leave. To follow *him*. They couldn't hang around in that atmosphere anymore, so they followed him to New Salem, with all their tools—including the Master Tools."

"You told me that he was a leader of the original coven," Cassie said. "But I wonder if he was a leader before the coven moved to New Salem—or only after."

The faces of the Circle members were very sober.

"I think he's trying to do the same thing again," Adam said. "Turn everybody against us so we don't have anywhere else to go—but to him. He's the only one who can defend us."

"He can go to hell," Deborah said, as if this ought to be obvious.

"Yeah, well, I'm sure he doesn't think we're going to come crawling to him right now," Nick murmured. "Things may look a little different in a couple of weeks."

"I think we'd better have a talk with Faye," Diana said.

They lay in wait for Faye by the back entrance of the auditorium, where Deborah thought she was most likely to come out. When she did she had the clipboard on her arm.

"Alone at last," Nick said, and they surrounded her, the eleven of them, forcing her to a stop. Looking at the faces of the Circle members right then, Cassie was reminded of the way Faye, Deborah, and Suzan had looked when they had caught her spying on them in front of the school. Beautiful, focused, and deadly. Dangerous.

Faye looked around at them and tossed her head. It didn't work as well with her hair gathered up in a bun.

"Get out of my way. I have work to do," she said.

"For him?" Adam asked tightly. Diana laid a hand on his arm and spoke herself.

"Faye, we know you can't talk now. But

we're going to have a ceremony tonight, because it's the night of Hecate—"

"And our birthday," Chris put in, aggrieved.

"—and we want you to be there."

"*You're* going to have a ceremony?" Faye said, looking less like a rich man's girl Friday and more like her old self, the black panther. "You can't. I'm the coven leader."

"How can you be the coven leader when you're never even with the coven? We're going to have this ceremony tonight, Faye, at the crossroads of Crowhaven and Marsh Street. With or without you. If you're there, you're welcome to lead it."

Faye looked for backing from Deborah and Suzan, her age-old supporters. But the biker's petite face was set in a hard scowl and Suzan's china-blue eyes were blank. No help was coming from that quarter.

"Traitors," Faye said contemptuously. Her beautiful, sulky mouth pinched, but she said, "I'll be there—to *lead* the ceremony. Now you'd better get out of here before a hall monitor spots you."

She turned and stalked away.

They all managed to get through that day without serious trouble, although Suzan received a detention for not throwing away a cupcake wrapper. Not for leaving it at a table or anything, just for not throwing it away as soon as she was done eating. It was a Type-A infraction.

That night they celebrated the Henderson brothers' birthday quietly, at Adam's house. Chris and Doug were extremely disappointed. They wanted a beach party with skinny-dipping. "And all kinds of wildness," Chris said. Adam said it was this or nothing.

Faye showed up around ten, wearing the black raw-silk shift she'd worn the night of the leadership vote. "In my day it was white," old Mrs. Franklin chuckled, leading her into the untidy living room with its comfortable, shabby furniture. "But times change."

Faye didn't even answer her. "I'm here," she said with a haughty glance around. "Let's go."

Cassie studied the silver diadem nestled in Faye's midnight-dark hair, the silver bracelet on Faye's rounded arm, and the garter, made of green leather lined with sky-blue silk, on Faye's thigh. She wondered what the real ones, the ones used by the original coven, looked like.

There wasn't much talking as the seven girls walked slowly down Crowhaven Road. Diana and Faye were in the lead, and Cassie heard Diana speaking in a low voice. The blond girl was carrying a white bag that held the things necessary for casting a circle and beginning a meeting.

They reached the crossroads. "It has to be a junction where three roads diverge," Diana had said, "to symbolize the three stages of womanhood: maiden, mother, and crone." Here Marsh Street met Crowhaven Road running north and south.

"Do we have to be right *in* the road?" Suzan said now. "What if somebody comes driving up?"

"We get out of the way, fast," said Laurel.

"I think we're safe," Diana said. "There aren't many cars this late. Come on, you guys, it's cold."

"It's my ceremony," Faye reminded her, taking out the ritual black-handled knife.

"I never said it wasn't," Diana said quietly. She stepped back to watch Faye cast the circle. Cassie felt blood burning in her own face as she stood behind Diana, watching Faye do what Diana had always done, what Diana would still be doing—if not for Cassie. She wanted to whisper something to Diana but instead she just made the promise in her own heart.

Somehow I'll make things right. Faye won't be the leader forever. Whatever I have to do, I'll see to that, she thought. She added, almost absently, I swear by Earth, Water, Fire, and Air.

EIGHT

Faye drew a circle on the road with the black-handled knife. Then she went around the circle with water sprinkled from a cup, then with a long stick of incense, then with a lighted candle. Symbolizing the elements Cassie had named: Earth, Water, Air, and Fire. The sweet, pungent smell of the incense drifted to Cassie on the cool night air.

"All right, come inside," Faye said. They filed into the circle through a gap which faced northeast, and sat down around the inner perimeter. It was strange to see only the faces of girls around the circle, Cassie thought.

"Do you want to explain or shall I?" Diana asked Faye, her hand on the white bag. There was still something inside it.

"Oh, you can *explain*," Faye said negligently.

"All right. We each take a candle, you see, and light it, and put it in a circle in the middle. And we each say a word, naming one of the aspects of womanhood. Not the stages, you know, like maiden, mother, and crone, but a quality. A—"

"Virtue," Melanie helped her out.

"Right. A virtue. Something that women have. Then, when we get all of them together, we show the candles to the elements and get their blessing. It's an affirmation of what we girls are, sort of; a celebration."

"I think that's lovely," Cassie said softly.

"All right; let's do it. Who wants red, or do I need to ask?" Diana took a red candle out of the bag. Very faintly, Cassie thought she caught the warm, spicy scent of cinnamon.

"Me. I'm red," Faye said. She turned the candle over in her hands, examining its smooth waxiness. She held it upright and cupped a hand swiftly around the wick. Cassie saw the flame spring into being, shining through Faye's fingers so they looked like pink shells, turning Faye's long red nails into jewels.

Diana, who had been holding a pack of

134

matches toward Faye, put them down.

"Passion," Faye said throatily, smiling her old, slow smile around the group as she dripped wax on the road and stuck the candle in it.

"Is that a virtue?" Melanie asked skeptically.

Faye raised an eyebrow. "It's an aspect of womanhood. It's the one I want to celebrate."

"Let her have it," Laurel said. "Passion's okay."

The red candle burned like a star.

"Next comes orange," said Diana. "Who wants that?"

"I'll take it," Suzan said. The orange candle was close to the titian of Suzan's own hair. Suzan sniffed at it.

"Peaches," she said, and Cassie could smell the sweet, voluptuous fragrance from where she sat. "All right: beauty," Suzan said. She lit her candle in the conventional manner, with a match.

"Beauty *definitely* isn't—"

"Well, it's not a virtue, but it's something women have," Cassie argued. Melanie rolled her eyes. Suzan stuck the orange candle in its own wax on the road, beside the red one.

"Here, let me go next. *I* know how to do this," Deborah said. She snatched up the white sack and rummaged in it, coming out with a yellow candle.

"Matches," she said commandingly to Suzan, who put them in her outstretched palm. Deborah lit the yellow candle.

"Courage," she said, clearly and distinctly, tilting the candle so a transparent stream of yellow wax ran onto the road. Cassie smelled a clean lemony sharpness and thought that it smelled like Deborah, like courage. The flame of the yellow candle lit Deborah's dark hair and flickered madly off her leather jacket as it burned by the other two.

"Okay, green," Diana said, retrieving the bag.

"Me," said Melanie, and took the dark green candle. She was sitting right beside Cassie and Cassie leaned in to smell the wax when Melanie did. It was scented with something woodsy: pine, Cassie decided. Like a Christmas tree.

"Wisdom," said Melanie, her cool gray eyes steady as she lit the wick. She breathed in the scent for a moment, then placed the green candle on the road. The four burning candles formed a semicircle.

"Now blue," said Diana. Cassie felt a jolt of nervousness and excitement. Blue was her favorite color, and she wanted it, but she wasn't quite sure she ought to speak out. Still, Diana and Laurel weren't saying anything, and she remembered that Laurel liked amethysts and often wore purple. Cassie cleared her throat.

"I'll take it," she said, and reached for the pale blue candle Diana offered. She was very pleased to have it, to represent blue in the coven's rainbow—but she hadn't thought of anything to say. What's blue like? she asked herself, sniffing at the candle to gain time. What virtue do girls have that I want to celebrate?

She couldn't quite identify the scent, which was sweet but sharp. "It's bayberry," Melanie told her, as Cassie kept sniffing. "A smell with a history. The colonists all used to make bayberry candles."

"Oh." Maybe that was why it smelled familiar. Maybe her grandmother had burned bayberry candles—her grandmother had done a lot of old-fashioned things. Cassie knew what virtue she wanted to celebrate now.

"Inspiration," she said. "That's imagination— or like the flash of an idea, you know. When my grandmother was helping make my muse outfit for Halloween, she said that's what the muses were for. They gave people inspiration, the ability to think of new things, to have brilliant ideas. And they were female, the muses."

Cassie hadn't meant to make a speech, and she looked down, embarrassed. I didn't get the matches, she realized—and then she had an inspiration. Cupping her hand around the candlewick as Faye had, she concentrated hard, thinking of fire, bright leaping fire—then she *pushed* with her mind, the way she had with the doberman and with Sean. She felt the power leave her like a blast of heat and focus on the wick and suddenly a flame shot up, so high that she had to jerk her hand away to keep from getting burned.

"An idea—just like that," she said, a little shaken, and she dripped wax on the road to stick the blue candle in. The other girls were looking at her wide-eyed, except Faye, whose eyes were narrow and hooded.

Deborah grinned. "I guess we've got more than one fire-handler around here," she said. Faye looked even less amused.

"Ah—purple," Diana said, giving herself a little shake and taking a lavender candle from the bag.

"That's me. How did you *do* that, Cassie? All right; I'm going on with the ceremony. I just wanted to know," Laurel said. She looked at her candle. "I don't know how to get mine into one word," she said. "I wanted to do environmental awareness—sort of like, *connectedness* to all things. We're a part of the earth and we should care about all the other things that live here with us."

"What about 'compassion'?" Melanie said quietly. "That would cover it, I think."

"That's good; compassion." Laurel lit the purple candle.

"What's it smell like?" Suzan whispered as Laurel stuck the candle in the road between Cassie's blue candle and Faye's red one, completing the rainbow circle.

"It's sweet and floral; I think it's supposed to be hyacinth," Laurel whispered back.

"Wait," Cassie said. "If it goes there, what about Diana? Don't you get a candle, Diana?" She felt jealous on Diana's behalf, she wanted the blond girl to have a turn too.

"Yes: white goes in the middle, and I'm the only one left to do it." And it's perfect, Cassie thought, watching Diana take out the vanilla-scented white candle and hold it up. Diana represented white as surely as Faye did red.

It showed in the virtue Diana named, too. "Purity," she said simply, lighting the white candle with a match and reaching into the circle of candles to place it in the center. Anybody else would have sounded ridiculous saying it, but Diana looked like the embodiment of purity sitting there, her beautiful face lit by the candles, her silky straight hair of that impossible color falling down her back. Her expression was serious and unself-conscious. When Diana said purity she *meant* purity, and not even Faye dared to snicker.

The circle of candles was pretty; seven tongues of flame leaping and dancing in the night air; seven scents mingling into one delicious composite fragrance. Eddies in the breeze seemed to bring the smell of cinnamon to Cassie, then a whiff of pine, then the sharpness of lemon.

"Passion, beauty, courage, wisdom, inspiration, compassion, and purity," Laurel ticked off, pointing to the candles that represented each.

"Let us all . . ." Diana prompted, nudging Faye.

"Let us all have all of them," Faye said. "Earth, Water, Fire, Air, witness. Not that we don't have them already," she added, regarding the glowing circle with a satisfied smile. Laurel's eyes twinkled at Cassie from across the flames and Cassie let her own eyes twinkle back.

"Well, anyway, we have all of them if you count all of *us*," Deborah said, and grinned. Diana smiled her gentle smile. For a moment, all the girls were smiling at each other over the candles, and Cassie felt as if they were a part of something bigger. Each of them contributed something important, and together they were more than just the sum of the parts.

"Now we're supposed to let them burn all night," Melanie said, nodding at the candles.

"What if somebody runs them over?" Suzan asked pragmatically.

"Well, I guess if we don't see it, it doesn't matter," Diana said. "Wait, though, there's something else I wanted to do. It's not part of the night of Hecate, but it's another Greek thing, the Arretophoria. It means the trust festival." She reached into the white bag again. "The Greek priestesses of Athena used to do this. It's where one of the older members of the group—that's me—gives a box to the youngest member—that's you, Cassie. You have to go bury the box somewhere without looking at what's inside it. It's supposed to be a dark and perilous journey you go on, but I think Nick's right and you'd better stick around here. Just

141

take it off the road somewhere and bury it."

"And that's all?" Cassie looked at the box Diana had given her. It was made of some light-colored wood, carved all over with tiny, intricate figures: bees and bears and fish. Something inside it rattled. "I just bury it?"

"That's all," Diana said, handing Cassie the last item from the white bag: a small trowel. "The point is that you don't look inside it. That's why it's called the trust festival; it's a celebration of trust and responsibility and friendship. Someday later we'll come back and dig it up."

"Okay." Carrying the box and trowel, Cassie stepped outside the circle and walked away from the group, leaving the little dancing points of flame behind.

She didn't want to bury the box close to the road. For one thing, the soil was hard and strewn with gravel; it wouldn't be easy to dig here; she'd just be scratching at the surface. Besides, this close someone might see the ground had been disturbed and dig the box up before its time.

Cassie kept walking east. She could hear the whispering of the sea from that direction and feel a faint, salty breeze. She climbed over some large rocks, and the beach stretched out before her, deserted and somehow eerie. Lacy white waves were lapping quietly at the shore.

A yellow moon, just over half full, was rising above the ocean. The mourning moon, Cassie remembered. It was just the color of Faye's eyes. In fact, it looked like a jaundiced, ancient eye, and Cassie had the uncomfortable sense of being spied on as she stuck the trowel into the cold dry sand and began to dig.

That was deep enough. The sand scooped out by the trowel was caked now, and she hoped the moisture wouldn't ruin Diana's box. As Cassie put the wooden box in the hole, moonlight glinted off the brass hasp. It wasn't locked. For just an instant, she had the temptation to open it.

Don't be *stupid*, she told herself. After all you and Diana have been through, if you can't do a little thing like bury a box without looking inside . . .

Nobody would know, the voice in her mind countered defensively.

I would know, Cassie told the voice. So there. She dumped sand on the box decisively, scooping with both the trowel and her hand to cover it faster.

It was sometime while she was covering the box that she noticed the blackness.

It's just a shadow, she thought. The moon was high enough now to throw a long shadow behind an outcrop of rock which was closer to the water than Cassie. Cassie watched it out of the corner of her eye as she smoothed the sand over the buried box. There, now you'd never know anything was hidden here. The shadow was stretching closer, but that was just because the moon was rising . . .

Wrong, Cassie thought. She stopped in the middle of brushing sand off her hands and looked at it.

Shadows get *shorter* as the moon gets higher. Just like the sun, she thought. But this one was definitely closer to her.

The whispering of the ocean was suddenly loud.

I should have listened to Diana. I should have stayed near the group, Cassie thought. Slowly and casually, she glanced over her shoulder. The rocks she'd climbed over seemed far away, and there was no sign of the circle of candles behind them. No sound either, except the waves. Cassie felt exposed and very much alone.

Don't act scared. Get up and go, she told

herself. Her heart was knocking against her ribs. As she stood, the shadow moved.

Oh God. There was no way to pretend that was normal. The shadow wasn't even attached to the rock anymore. It was just a blackness on the sand, flowing like water, moving toward her. It was alive.

Go, go! Cassie's mind screamed at her. But her legs wouldn't obey. They were locked, paralyzed. She wasn't going anywhere.

Cassssie. Her head jerked up; she looked for the person who had spoken. But it wasn't a person. It was the waves.

Casssssie.

I want to get out of here, Cassie thought. Her legs still wouldn't move.

The blackness flowed like tar, rippling toward her. It divided, pouring itself on either side of her, encircling her.

Casssssie.

The shadow was whispering to her with Black John's voice. It eddied around her, a formless darkness like smoke. As she looked down at it, Cassie seemed to see snakes in it, and black beetles, all crawling loathsome things. It was around her, but it didn't want to kill her. It wanted to get into her mind.

She could *feel* it trying. A pressure as it swirled around her feet. All she could think was, thank God I don't still have the hematite.

I should have listened; why didn't I listen? she thought then. The girls wouldn't miss her for a while. Too long. She wanted to scream, but her throat was as paralyzed as her legs. She could only stand there and watch the rippling blackness swirl around her feet.

Push with your mind, she thought, but she was too frightened. She couldn't scare away this darkness the way she had the doberman. She wasn't strong enough.

Please help me, she thought.

And then, in a rush, it was all she was thinking. Oh please somebody help me, somebody please come, I can't get out of this myself, oh please *somebody*—

Casssssssie, the whisper came. The waves and the darkness and the watching moon all seemed to be saying it.

Help me . . .

"Cassie!" It was a shout, not a whisper, and behind it Cassie heard a dog barking. At the sound, Cassie's mind was flooded with images of safety, of comfort. She looked around frantically. Her legs still wouldn't move.

"I'm here!" she shouted back. Even as she called, she felt herself released. The black was edging away, retreating to the rock. Merging with the real shadow there.

"Cassie!" The voice was familiar, loved.

"I'm here," Cassie called again, stumbling toward it. The visions of comfort and safety and closeness were still whirling inside her, pulling her. She followed them. Just as she reached the rocks, strong arms caught her up, held her tightly. She felt the warmth of a human body against her.

Over Nick's shoulder, she met Adam's eyes.

The moon was shining full in his face, turning those eyes odd colors, blue-violet like the bottom of a flame. Like the sky before some strange storm. She thought she could see silver reflecting in his pupils. Raj bounded up beside him, still barking. The German shepherd's tail was waving frantically as he headed for Cassie. Adam caught him by the ruff and held him back.

"Are you okay? Are you hurt?" Nick said in her ear.

"No. I'm all right," she whispered. She didn't know what she was saying.

"You shouldn't have gone off by yourself,"

Nick said angrily. "They shouldn't have let you do it."

"It's okay, Nick." She hung on to him with all her strength and buried her face in his shoulder just as Adam turned, leading the reluctant Raj away. Then she clung there, knowing he could feel her shaking.

"Cassie." He stroked her back soothingly.

Cassie pulled back slightly. Adam was gone. She looked at Nick in the moonlight, at the clean carven handsomeness of his features with their hint of coldness. Except his eyes weren't cold now.

Passion, she thought and brought up Faye's red candle in her mind. Then she kissed him.

She'd never really kissed anybody besides Adam, but she guessed she knew how to do it well enough. Nick's mouth was warm, and that was nice. She felt how startled he was, and then instantly felt the surprise swept away by something deeper, sweeter. She felt him kissing her back.

She kissed not to think. Kissing was good for that. Suzan had been dead wrong about Nick. He wasn't an iguana. Little lines of fire ran along Cassie's nerves, tingling her fingers. She felt warm all over.

Eventually, they both broke it. Cassie looked up at him, her fingers still intermeshed with his.

"Sorry," she said unsteadily. "I was just scared."

"Remind me to get you scared frequently," Nick said. He looked slightly dazed.

"We'd better go back. Black John was here."

She had to give Nick credit; he didn't yell *"What?"* and shake her. He cast a quick, hunting look around, switching his grip on her so that he was holding her arm with his left hand and his right hand was free.

"He's gone now," she said. "There was a shadow that came out from that rock, but it's not there anymore."

"After this, nobody goes out alone," Nick said, guiding her toward the rocks they had to climb to get back to the crossroads.

"I think he was trying to get into my mind," Cassie told the others when they were all back at Adam's house again. She sat beside Nick, holding tightly to his hand. "To influence me, or take me over, or whatever. I didn't know how to stop him. If you guys hadn't come, he would have done it."

"Nobody should be out by themselves anymore," Nick said, with a hard glance at

Diana. It was unlike Nick to say anything at meetings, but now his voice was decisive, not to be argued with.

"I agree," said Melanie. "Moreover, I think we should do something to defend ourselves, to put up some kind of shield against him."

"What did you have in mind?" Adam asked her. He was sitting on the arm of Diana's chair, his face calm, his voice steady.

"Some kind of crystal might help. Amethyst, maybe. It should help us to focus and fight against him, against any psychic attack. Of course, if anyone were simultaneously wearing another crystal that he could use against them—like hematite—it wouldn't do any good." Melanie was looking at Faye.

Faye made an impatient gesture. "As I've already told my interfering cousin, I don't have any stupid hematite. I don't have to steal other people's crystals."

"All right; we won't argue," Diana said. "Melanie, do you have enough amethysts at your place? Or can you lend us some, Laurel? I think we should get them ready immediately, so everybody can wear them home tonight."

"Yes, and keep them on all the time," Melanie said. "When you take a bath, when you go to sleep, at school, whatever. But wear them under your clothes; don't let him see the crystals, if possible. They'll be more effective that way."

"What a way to end a party," Doug groused, as he picked up his jacket.

"Think of it as a party favor," Nick replied unsympathetically. "A memento." He squeezed Cassie's fingers quickly with a sideways glance, as if to say he knew what *he* would be remembering.

Cassie felt warmed by that. But as they were leaving for Melanie's house she asked casually, "By the way, why *did* you guys come after me?"

"Yeah, did you get bored with the party or something? Found out you couldn't deal all by yourselves, so you had to find us girls?" Deborah put in, her dark eyes flashing at Chris.

Chris looked at her oddly. "No, we were dealin' fine. It was Adam who told us to come. He said Cassie was in trouble."

NINE

Cassie's piece of amethyst was quite large. It was a pendant, hanging from the claws of a silver owl with outspread wings, and it felt cool against Cassie's chest under her blue and white sweater. She checked in Diana's mirror to make sure it didn't make a bump and then touched it nervously. Cassie had had three stones so far: the chalcedony rose Adam had given her, the quartz necklace Melanie had put around her neck at the Homecoming dance, and the piece of hematite she'd found at Number Thirteen. She hadn't kept any of them long. The chalcedony she'd had to give back to Adam, the quartz had been lost that same night at the burying ground, and the hematite had been stolen. She just hoped nothing was going to happen to this amethyst.

Clouds had gathered in the night, and the sky was steely-gray as Diana drove them to school that morning. And school these days was about as bleak as the weather. Hall monitors, wearing badges and wintry expressions, stood in every corridor waiting for someone to break the rules. Which usually didn't take very long; there were so many rules that it was impossible not to break one or two just by being alive.

"We almost got sent up for wearing a noisemakin' device," Chris said as they were walking down the hall at lunchtime.

Cassie tensed. "What did you do?"

"Bribed him," Doug said with a wicked grin. "We gave him a Walkman."

"My Walkman," Chris said, aggrieved.

"I wonder what the penalty for bribing a hall monitor is?" Laurel mused as they reached the cafeteria.

Cassie opened her mouth, but the words froze on her lips. Through the glass windows of the cafeteria she could see something that wiped all thought from her mind.

"Oh *God*," said Laurel.

"I don't believe it," Diana whispered.

154

"I do," Adam said.

In the very center of the cafeteria was a wooden structure that Cassie recognized from her history books. It was made in two parts, which when closed held a person's wrists and neck securely in place, protruding through holes from the other side.

The stocks.

And they were occupied.

There was a guy inside them, a big husky guy Cassie recognized from her algebra class. He'd danced with her at Homecoming, and he'd been overly familiar with his hands. He liked to talk back to teachers, too. But she'd never seen him do anything deserving of *this*.

"He won't get away with it," Diana was saying, her green eyes blazing with intensity.

"Who, the principal?" Deborah asked. She and Suzan and Nick were standing by the cafeteria door, waiting for the others. "He already has. He was taking some parents on a guided tour a few minutes ago and they came through here . . . he *showed* it to them, for God's sake. Said it was part of a 'tough love' program. Said other schools made troublemakers stand on tables so everybody could look at them, but that he thought the stocks were more humane because you could sit down. He almost made it sound *reasonable*. And they were just nodding and smiling—they ate it up."

Cassie felt queasy. She was thinking of the Witch Dungeon at Salem, where she and Chris and Doug had scuttled through narrow corridors lined with tiny dark cells. The stocks gave her the same sick feeling in her stomach. How can people do this to other people? she thought.

"—passing it off as part of our heritage," Nick was saying, his lip curled in disgust, and Cassie knew he felt the same way.

"Can we talk about it while we eat?" Suzan asked, shifting from one foot to the other. "I'm starving."

But as they made their way toward the back room—the private domain of the Club for the last four years—a short figure with rusty hair stepped in front of them.

"Sorry," Sally Waltman smirked. "That room is for hall monitors only, now."

"Oh, yeah?" said Deborah.

Two guys with badges appeared from nowhere and stood on either side of Sally.

"Yeah," one of them said.

Cassie looked through the glass windows of the back room—there was no crowd of hangers-on standing in front of it today—and saw Portia's tawny head. She was surrounded by girls and guys who were looking at her admiringly. They all wore badges.

"You'll just have to sit somewhere else," Sally was telling the Club. "And since there aren't enough seats at any one table, you'll have to break your group up. What a shame."

"We'll go outside," Nick said shortly, taking Cassie's arm.

Sally laughed. "I don't think so. No more eating out front. If you can't find a place to sit in here, you stand."

Cassie could feel Nick's muscles cord. She held on to his arm tightly. Diana had a similar hold on Adam, whose blue-gray eyes were like chips of steel, fixed on the guys beside Sally.

"It's not worth it," Diana said quietly, with forced calm. "It's what he wants. Let's go stand over there."

Sally looked disappointed as they all started to move to the wall. Then triumph flashed in her eyes.

"*He's* in violation already," she said, pointing to Doug. "He's wearing a radio."

"It's not on," Doug said.

"It doesn't have to be. Just wearing it is a

Type-A offense. Come with me, please." The two guys surged forward to help Doug come.

"Nick, don't. Wait—" Cassie gasped, getting in front of him. A fight in the cafeteria was all they needed.

Doug's eyes were glittering wildly. He looked mad enough to hit Sally, not to mention the two guys.

"Bring him," Sally said in an exultant voice. The guys reached for Doug. Doug's fist jerked back. And then a throaty voice cut through the confusion.

"What's going on here?" Faye said, her amber eyes smoldering. She was wearing another of the little business suits; this one black and yellow.

Sally glared at her. "They're refusing to comply with the orders of a hall monitor," she said. "And *he's* wearing a radio."

Faye reached over and unhooked the Walkman from Doug's belt. "Now he's not," she said. "And I'm telling them to go eat somewhere else—outside, maybe. On *my* authority."

Sally was sputtering. Faye chuckled and led the Club out of the cafeteria.

"Thanks," Diana said, and for a moment she and Faye looked each other in the eye. Cassie thought of the candles burning in a circle on the road. A new stage of life—was Faye entering a new stage of life? Coming back to the coven?

But Faye's next words undeceived her. "You know, there's no reason that you *can't* eat in the back room," she said. "You can all become hall monitors. That's what he wants—"

"He wants to take us over," interrupted Deborah scornfully.

"He wants to join with us. He's one of us."

"No, he's not, Faye," Cassie said, thinking of the shadow under the rock. "He's nothing like us."

Faye gave her a strange glance, but all she said was, "There's a hall monitors' meeting in C-207 last period. Think about it. The sooner you join him, the easier things will be." She tossed Doug's Walkman back to him with a negligent gesture and walked away.

Lunch was uncomfortable; it was cold in the front yard of the school, and nobody but Suzan had much of an appetite. Sean showed up late, after all the excitement was over. They discussed plans to fight Black John, but as always they came back to the single issue of power. They needed power to fight him effectively. They needed the Master Tools.

Everyone had a different idea of where to

search. Adam proposed the beach—especially around Devil's Cove, where Mr. Fogle, the former principal, had been killed by a rock slide. Deborah thought maybe the old burying ground. "It's been here since the 1600s," she said. "The original coven could easily have hidden things there." Melanie and Diana discussed the possibility of making a crystal pendulum designed to seek out traces of "white energy" the tools might be giving off.

Cassie sat quietly, close to Nick, not saying much. She had the stupid, desperate urge to forget all of this and bury her head in his shoulder. She didn't know New Salem as well as the others—how could she come up with a reasonable place to search? And she had such a feeling of dread, of evil things just waiting to happen.

We're going to lose, she thought, listening to the worried voices of the others. We're just kids, and he's got centuries of experience. We're going to lose.

The feeling of dread got worse as the day went on. She ran into Nick as she was walking to her last class and he stopped in the hall.

"You look awful," he said.

"Thanks." Cassie tried a wry smile for him.

"No, I mean you're so pale—you feeling okay? Do you want to go home?"

"Leaving school grounds without permission," Cassie quoted automatically, tiredly, and then she was in his arms.

Nick said, "They can take their permission and—"

Cassie just clung to him. Nick was so good to her; she wanted to love him. She would *make* herself love him, she decided. Maybe they should go back to Crowhaven Road; go someplace where they could be alone. Nick didn't like doing this kind of thing where people could see.

"Hold me," she said. He did. Then he kissed her.

Yes. Just go with it. Be part of Nick—that was safe. Nick would take care of her. She could stop thinking now.

"Well, well, well . . . looks like a Type-A violation to *me*," an officious voice said. "Public displays of affection, inappropriate to the serious and dignified purpose of formal education. What do you say, Portia?"

Nick and Cassie broke apart, Cassie flushing.

"I think it's just too revolting," Portia Bainbridge said.

161

Behind her was a gaggle of hall monitors, on their way to the meeting, apparently. There were maybe thirty of them. Cassie's heart was suddenly beating hard and fast.

"And it's *her* fault," Portia went on, looking down her aristocratic nose at Cassie. "I heard her initiate it. Let's take her in."

"That's right, the little flirt," Sally said. Cassie remembered Sally's voice in the bathroom; the anger in it, the viciousness. *This one had every guy at Homecoming dance following her around with his tongue hanging out—including my boyfriend.* She'd come to think of herself so differently since she'd overheard Sally talking about her that day.

Nick was looking at the group of monitors, his face cold—like the old Nick, the one Cassie had first met. Cold as ice. "Take her where? The penalty for a Type-A offense is supposed to be detention. Or don't you read your own rules?" he said.

"*We* decide what the penalties are—" Portia began, but Sally interrupted.

"She was refusing to cooperate with a hall monitor at lunchtime," she said. "That's what we're taking her in for. Mr. Brunswick gave us special instructions. We're going to take her to

162

the office—she can talk to *him*."

"Then you can take both of us," Nick said. His arm tightened on Cassie.

There were too many of them. Cassie's eyes skimmed over the crowd of hall monitors, seeing not a friendly face among them. All seniors, all kids who hated witches. And Faye wasn't here now.

"Nick," she said, her voice soft and careful over the thumping of her heart, "I think I'd better go with them." She glanced back at Sally. "Can I just say good-bye to him?"

Looking sardonic, Sally nodded. Cassie put her arms around Nick's neck.

"Get the others," she whispered in his ear. "The monitors will be in their meeting—you'll have to find a way to get me out."

As he drew back, Nick's mahogany eyes met hers in acknowledgement. Then, with an expressionless look at Sally, he stood aside.

The group of monitors surrounded Cassie and escorted her down the hall, treating her like a mass murderer. She had a wild impulse to giggle, but as they reached the office the urge disappeared in a flood of sheer dread and anxiety.

He planned this, she thought. Maybe not this specifically, today. But he knew he'd get us somehow, one by one. She tried to ignore the little voice whispering, *he knew he'd get you. It's you he's after.*

Because she was an outsider—or because she didn't fit in with his plans. A vision of Kori flashed through her mind: Kori lying stiff and motionless with a broken neck at the bottom of the hill. She'd seen what happened to people who didn't fit in with Black John's plans.

"Maybe if you bat your eyes at him he'll let you off," Sally whispered spitefully and pushed her in the office door.

Cassie didn't answer. She couldn't.

She hadn't been in this office since she'd gone to Mr. Fogle to complain that Faye was persecuting her. It looked the same, except that there was a crackling fire in the fireplace now. And the man behind the desk was different.

Don't look at him, Cassie thought, as the door swung shut behind her, but she couldn't help it. Those black eyes held hers from the instant she glanced toward the desk. That hawklike face betrayed no sign of surprise that she was there.

The principal put a slim gold-plated pen on the desk with a barely audible click.

"Cassandra," he said.

Cassie's knees felt weak.

It was the voice of the shadow. A dark, liquid voice. So quiet, so insidious—so *evil*. Under his hematite-black eyes she felt naked, exposed. As if he were looking at her mind. Looking for a crack to get in.

"Mr. Brunswick," she said. Her voice sounded strange to her own ears. Polite, but distant.

He smiled.

He was wearing a black turtleneck and a black jacket. He stood, resting his fingertips on the desk.

"So brave," he said. "I'm proud of you."

It was the last thing she expected. Cassie just stared at him. Her fingers flew automatically to the bump of the amethyst pendant under her sweater.

His eyes followed the movement. "I wouldn't bother," he said, smiling faintly. "That crystal is much too small to be effective."

Cassie's hand dropped slowly. How had he known? She felt so confused, so off-balance. She stared at the man in front of her, trying to connect him with the burned creature that had crouched over her grandmother in the kitchen, with the seventeenth-century wizard who had led a frightened coven to New Salem. How was he here at all, that was the question. What was the source of his power?

"And amethyst is a weak stone, a stone of the heart," he was going on softly. "Purity of purpose, Cassie; that's the secret. Purity and clarity. Never forget your purpose."

She had the strange feeling he was answering her question. Oh God, why didn't Nick come? Her heart was pounding so hard . . . she was *frightened*.

"Let me demonstrate," the dark man said. "If you would give me that pendant? For a moment only," he added, as Cassie stood motionless.

Slowly, Cassie reached around the back of her neck. With cold fingertips she undid the silver chain and removed it. She didn't know what else to do.

Slowly, precisely, he took it.

Suddenly, wildly, Cassie thought of a magician about to do a trick. Nothing up *those* sleeves, she thought. Only flesh that shouldn't be there in the first place.

Still holding the necklace in the air, the principal turned away from Cassie. The fire leaped and crackled and Cassie felt her pulse in her throat and fingertips. I can't stand much more of this, she thought. Nick, where are you?

"You see," the principal said, in a voice that

seemed oddly distorted, "amethyst is a stone riddled with impurities. For power, quartz is always my choice . . ." He began to turn around.

No, thought Cassie. Everything had gone into slow motion, as if she were watching one frame after another of a video. A video played on a very superior machine, each frame crisp and bright and sharp-edged, with no blurriness. Cassie didn't even know where the *No* had come from, except that something deep in her own brain was screaming in protest, trying to warn her. Don't look, oh, don't look.

Cassie wanted to stop the action, to freeze the frame. But she couldn't. It was taking forever, but the dark man was still turning. He was facing her.

She saw the elegant black jacket, the black turtleneck sweater. But above the turtleneck was a monstrosity that forced tears from her eyes and clogged the scream in her throat. The man had no face.

No hair, no eyebrows, no eyes, no nose. No mouth, only a grinning outline of clenched teeth. Even that, even the stark bones which faced her, were as clear as water.

Cassie couldn't scream, couldn't breathe. Her mind was out of control.

Oh God, oh God the skull isn't gone no wonder we couldn't find it, it didn't explode at all because it's in his head, oh Diana oh Adam it's in his *head* . . .

"You see, Cassandra," came the inhuman voice from behind those clenched teeth, "purity plus clarity equals power. And I have more power than you children have ever dreamed of."

Oh God I won't believe this I won't believe this is happening I don't want to see any more . . .

"My spirit is not confined to this body," the voice went on calmly, with terrible lucidity. "It can flow like water wherever I direct it. I can focus its power anywhere."

The hollow eyesockets tilted down, toward the amethyst pendant which hung from a perfectly normal-looking hand. Firelight flickered deep inside the crystal. Then Cassie felt it—an outrush of power like the one she'd sent to scare the dog and to warn Sean and to light the match. Only this was much stronger, much more concentrated than her feeble bursts had been. She could almost *see* it, like a blaze of light.

The amethyst pendant shattered.

The silver owl swung, but nothing hung from its claws now. The crystal was gone.

Cassie's ears caught the tinkle as bits of it fell. But she didn't really notice the sound consciously. She was blind and deaf with panic.

"Now, Cassandra," the voice was beginning again, and then it was interrupted by a noise so loud that even Cassie couldn't ignore it. A *roar* was coming from the front yard of the school, a sound like a pep rally, only angry. Shrill screams rang out against the background of deep shouting.

The principal dropped the silver chain and strode over to the window which overlooked the front of the school.

And Cassie's brain woke up. It wanted only one thing, to get out of here. With the dark man's attention distracted, she dove for the door.

She ran straight through the office without looking at the secretaries. There was chaos in the second-floor halls. Everyone was flooding out of classrooms. "It's a fight!" some guy on the stairs was yelling. "Come on!"

It's like a riot; they can't control everybody at once, Cassie realized dimly. She was still running. She ran down the stairs and then down a hallway, instinctively heading for the center of the confusion.

"Cassie, wait!"

Not a man's voice, but a threatening one. Faye. Cassie paused for an instant, looking around desperately for Nick or Diana or Adam.

"Cassie, stop, for pity's sake. No one is trying to hurt you. I've been running after you all the way from the office."

Warily, Cassie edged backward. The hall was deserted now. Everyone was outdoors.

"Cassie, just *listen* to me. He's not trying to murder you, I promise. He wants to *help* you. He likes you."

"Faye, you're insane!" Cassie's control broke, and she screamed the words. "You don't know what he is! Everything you see about him is an illusion. He's a monster!"

"Don't be ridiculous. He's one of us—"

"Oh, my God, oh, my God," Cassie said. Reaction was setting in and her knees were shaking so badly that she had to lean against the wall. She slid down, tearing a poster about the Thanksgiving football game. "You didn't see him. You don't know."

"I know you're being a baby. *You* didn't even stay to listen to what he had to say to you. He was going to explain everything—"

"Faye, wake up!" Cassie cried. "For God's sake, will you please wake up and *look* at him?

He's nothing that you think. You're completely blind."

"You think you know so much about it." Faye stood back, arms crossed over her chest. She tilted her chin up and looked down at Cassie with heavy-lidded, queerly triumphant eyes. Her blood-red lips curved in a smile. "You think you know everything—but you don't even know what his name was when he was here last. When he came to our parents and he lived at Number Thirteen."

The strength of terror Cassie had felt moments earlier was gone, and the ground suddenly felt very unstable. She pressed a hand against the floor. Faye was still looking at her with those strange, triumphant eyes. "No," Cassie whispered.

"'No' you don't know? Or 'no' don't tell you? But I want to tell you, Cassie, and it's time you did know. The name he used last time was John Blake."

O

TEN

Cassie stared, beyond speech, beyond thought. Not believing—but inside her, something knew.

"It's true. He's your father."

Cassie just sat.

"And he wants you to be happy, Cassie. He wants you to be his heir. He's got a lot planned for you."

"And what are you?" Cassie cried, outraged, pushed beyond the limits of her endurance. "My new stepmother?"

Faye chuckled—that infuriating, lazy, self-satisfied chuckle. "Maybe. Why not? I've always liked older men—and he's only about three centuries older."

"You're disgusting!" Cassie couldn't find the

right words. None were bad enough, and she didn't want to believe that any of this was actually happening. "You're—you—"

"I haven't *done* anything yet, Cassie. John and I have a— business relationship."

Cassie felt as if she were gagging. For herself, for Faye . . . "You call him John?" she whispered.

"What do you think I should call him? Mr. Brunswick? Or what he called himself the last time he was here, Mr. Blake?"

Everything was spinning around Cassie now. The pale green cinderblock walls were whirling. She wanted to faint. If only she could faint she wouldn't have to think.

But she couldn't. Slowly, the spinning steadied; she felt the floor solid beneath her. There was no way to escape this. There was no choice but to deal with it.

"Oh, God," Cassie whispered. "It's true. It's really true."

"It's true," Faye said quietly, with satisfaction. "Your mother was his girlfriend. He told me the whole story, how she fell in love with him when he went over to Number Twelve to borrow some matches. They never *did* get married, apparently—but I'm sure he didn't begrudge her his name."

It was true . . . and that had been what Cassie's grandmother was trying to tell her when she died. "I have one more thing to tell you," she'd said, and then Laurel had come in. The last words had only been a whisper, "John" and something else Cassie couldn't make out. But she could recall the shape of her grandmother's lips trying to make it. It had been "Blake."

"Why didn't she try to tell me before?" Cassie whispered raggedly, hardly aware she was speaking aloud. "Why wait until she was dying? *Why?*"

"Who, your grandma? She didn't want to upset you, I suppose," Faye said. "She probably thought you'd be—disturbed—if you knew. And maybe"—Faye leaned forward—"she knew it would bring you closer to him. You're his own flesh and blood, Cassie. His daughter."

Cassie was shaking her head, blind, nauseated. "The other old women—they must have known too! God, everybody who knew him must have known. And *nobody* told me. Why didn't they tell me?"

"Oh, stop sniveling, Cassie. I'm sure they didn't tell you because they were afraid of how you'd react. And I must say it looks as if they were right. You're falling apart."

Great-aunt Constance, Cassie was thinking. *She* must have known. How could she stand to look at me? How can she stand to have my mother in her house?

And Mrs. Franklin had been *going* to tell her, she realized suddenly. Yes. That had been what that last-minute scene in Aunt Constance's parlor had been all about. Adam's grandmother had been about to tell, about to say something to Cassie about her father. Granny Quincey and Aunt Constance had stopped her. They were all in a conspiracy of silence, to keep the truth from Cassie.

Probably not the parents, Cassie thought slowly, feeling very tired. They probably didn't remember anyway. They'd made themselves forget everything. But Aunt Constance had warned the Circle against stirring up those old memories, and her gaze had settled on Cassie when she did it.

"Just think about it, Cassie," Faye was saying, and that husky voice sounded reasonable now, not gloating or triumphant. "He only wants the best for you; he always has. You were born as part of his plans. I know you and I have had our problems in the past, but John wants us to get along. Won't you just give it a try? Won't you, Cassie?"

Slowly, painfully, Cassie made her eyes focus. Faye was kneeling in front of her. Faye's beautiful, sensual face seemed lit softly from within. She really means it, Cassie thought. She's sincere. Maybe she's in love with him.

And maybe, Cassie mused dizzily, I *should* think about it. So many things have changed since I came to New Salem—I'm not at all the person I used to be. The old, shy Cassie who never had a boyfriend and never had anything to say is gone. Maybe this is just another change, another stage of life. Maybe I'm at the crossroads.

She looked at Faye for a long moment, searching the depths of those amber eyes. Then, slowly, she shook her head.

No.

Even as she thought it, chill white determination flooded her. That was one road she would never take, no matter what happened. She would never become what Black John— what her *father*—wanted.

Without a word, without looking back, Cassie got up and walked away from Faye.

Outside, the melee was still going on. Cassie scanned the front entrance of the school and saw the weak November sun shining on a cascade of fair hair. She headed for it.

"Diana . . ."

"Cassie, thank God! When Nick told us you were alone in his office . . ." Diana's eyes widened. "Cassie, what's wrong?"

"I have to tell you something. At home. Can we go home now?" Cassie was holding on to Diana's hand.

Diana stared at her for another moment, then shook herself. "Yes. Of course. But Nick will be looking for you. He had the idea that we should start a fight on the first floor as a diversion; just grab a bunch of people and start swinging. All the guys did it, and Deborah and Laurel. They're all looking for you."

Cassie couldn't face any of them, especially Nick. Once he knew what she really was—what he'd held in his arms, what he'd kissed . . .

"Please, can't you just tell them I'm okay, but I need to go home?" Suzan was standing nearby; Cassie nodded at her. "Can't Suzan just tell them?"

"Yes. All right. Suzan, tell everybody I've taken Cassie home. They can stop the fight now." Diana led Cassie down the hill to the parking lot. They had barely reached Diana's car, though, when Adam appeared, running.

"The fight's breaking up—and I'm coming with you," he said. Cassie wanted to argue, but she didn't have the strength. Besides, Diana might need Adam there when Cassie told her the whole story.

Cassie nodded at Adam and he got in the car without further discussion. They drove to Diana's house and went up to Diana's room.

"Now tell us what happened before I have a heart attack," Diana said.

But it wasn't that easy. Cassie went over to the bay window, where sunlight was striking the prisms hanging there so that wedges of rainbow light bobbed and slid over the walls. She turned to look at the black and white prints on either side of the window; Diana's collection of Greek goddesses. There was proud Hera, queenly with her mane of pitch-black hair and her hooded, untamed eyes; there was Aphrodite, goddess of beauty, with her soft bosom exposed; there was fierce Artemis, the virgin huntress afraid of nothing. And here, on the other side, was Athena, the gray-eyed goddess of wisdom, and Persephone, fresh-faced and elfin and surrounded by blooming flowers. Last of all, in color, was the print of a goddess older than the Greek civilization, the great goddess Diana, who ruled the moon and stars and night. Diana, Queen of Witches.

"Cassie!"

"Sorry," Cassie whispered, and slowly turned to face her Diana. Who just now looked sick with suspense.

"I'm sorry," she said, more loudly. "I just don't know how to say this, I guess. But I know now why I was born so much later than all of you . . . or, actually, no, I don't." She pondered that a moment. "Not why I was so late. Unless he knew by then the coven was going to try to throw him out, so he thought he'd better have a back-up . . ." Cassie thought it over and shook her head. Adam and Diana were staring at her as if she'd gone crazy. "I guess I don't know everything. But I'm not half outsider, like we thought. That isn't why he's been after me; it's a completely different reason. We thought Kori and I spoiled his plans somehow . . . oh, *God*." Cassie stopped, feeling a pain like jagged glass shoot through her. Her eyes filled. "I think— God, it must be. I know why Kori died. Because of *me*. If she hadn't died, she would have joined the coven instead of me, and he didn't want that. *She* was the one he hadn't planned on. So he had to get rid of her." Another spasm of pain almost doubled Cassie over. She was afraid she might be sick.

"Sit down," Adam was saying urgently. They were both helping her to the bed.

"Don't . . . you don't know yet. You might not want to touch me."

"Cassie, for God's sake tell us what you're talking about. You're not making any sense."

"Yes, I am. I'm Black John's daughter."

In that instant, if either of them had loosened their grip on her or recoiled, Cassie felt she might have tried to jump out the window. But Diana's clear green eyes just widened, the pupils huge and bottomless. Adam's eyes turned silver.

"Faye told me, and it's true."

"It's not true," Adam said tightly.

"It's not true, and I'll kill her," Diana said. This, from gentle Diana, was astonishing.

They both went on holding Cassie. Diana was holding her from one side and Adam was on the other side, holding both of them, embracing their embrace. Cassie's shaking shook all three.

"It is true," Cassie whispered, trying to keep some grip on herself. She had to be calm now; she couldn't lose control. "It explains every-thing. It explains why I dreamed about him— him and the sinking ship. We're—connected, somehow. It explains why he keeps coming after me, like when we called him up at Halloween, and last night on the beach. He wants me to join him. Faye's in love with him. Just like my mother was."

Cassie shuddered. Adam and Diana just kept hanging on to her. Neither of them even flinched when she looked them in the face.

"It explains my *mother*," Cassie said thickly. "Why he went to our house that night when he came back, when we let him out of the grave. He went to see her—that's why she's like she is now. Oh, Diana, I have to go to her."

"In a minute," Diana said, her own voice husky with suppressed tears. "In a little while."

Cassie was thinking. No wonder her mother had run away from New Salem, no wonder there had always been helpless terror lurking at the back of her mother's eyes. How could you not be terrified when the man you loved turned out to be something from a nightmare? When you had to go away to have his baby, someplace where no one would ever know?

But she'd been brave enough to come back, and to bring Cassie. And now Cassie had to be brave.

There's nothing frightening in the dark if you just

face it. Cassie didn't know how she was going to face this, but she had to, somehow.

"I'm okay now," she whispered. "And I want to see my mom."

Diana and Adam were telegraphing things over her head.

"We're going with you," Diana said. "We won't go in the room if you don't want, but we're going to take you there."

Cassie looked at them: at Diana's eyes, dark as emeralds now, but full of love and understanding; and at Adam, his fine-boned face calm and steady. She squeezed their hands.

"Thank you," she said. "Thank you both."

Great-aunt Constance answered the door. She looked surprised to see them and a little flustered, which surprised Cassie in turn. She wouldn't have thought Melanie's aunt ever got flustered.

But as Cassie was going into the guest room, Granny Quincey and old Mrs. Franklin were coming out. Cassie looked at Laurel's frail great-grandmother, and at Adam's plump, untidy grandmother, and then at Aunt Constance.

"We were—trying one or two things to see if we could help your mother," Aunt Constance said, looking slightly uncomfortable. She coughed. "Old remedies," she admitted. "There may be some good in them. We'll be in the parlor if you need anything." She shut the door.

Cassie turned to look at the figure lying between Aunt Constance's starched white sheets. She went and knelt by the bedside.

Her mother's face was as pale as those sheets. Everything about her was white and black: white face, black hair, black lashes forming crescents on her cheeks. Cassie took her cold hand and only then realized she didn't have the first idea what to say.

"Mother?" she said, and then: "Mom? Can you hear me?"

No answer. Not a twitch.

"Mom," Cassie said with difficulty, "I know you're sick, and I know you're scared, but there's one thing you don't have to be scared of anymore. I know the truth. I know about my father."

Cassie waited, and she thought she saw the sheets over her mother's chest rise and fall a little more quickly.

"I know everything," she said. "And . . . if you're afraid I'll be mad at you or anything, you don't have to be. I understand. I've seen what he does to people. I saw what he did to Faye,

184

and she's stronger than you." Cassie was holding the cold hand so tightly she was afraid she was hurting it. She paused and swallowed.

"Anyway, I wanted to tell you that I know. And it'll all be over soon, and I'm going to make sure he doesn't ever hurt you again. I'm going to stop him somehow. I don't know how, but I will. I promise, Mom."

She stood up, still holding the soft, limp hand in hers and whispered, "If you're just scared, Mom, you can come back now. It's easier than running away; it is, really. If you face things they're not as bad."

Cassie waited again. She hadn't thought she was hoping for anything, but she must have been, because as the seconds ticked by and nothing happened her heart sank in disappointment. Just some little sign, that wasn't much to ask for, was it? But there was no little sign. For what seemed like the hundredth time that day, warmth filled Cassie's eyes.

"Okay, Mom," she whispered, and stooped to kiss her mother's cheek.

As she did, she noticed a thin string of some kind of fiber around her mother's neck. She pulled, and from the collar of her mother's nightgown emerged three small golden-brown stones strung on the twine.

Cassie tucked the necklace back in, waited one more second, and then left.

Can I face it if my mother dies like my grandma? she wondered as she shut the bedroom door. She didn't think so. But she was beginning to realize that she might have to.

In the parlor, Adam and Diana were drinking tea with the women.

"Who put the crystals around my mother's neck? And what are they?"

The old women looked at each other. It was Great-aunt Constance who answered.

"I did," she said. She cleared her throat. "They're tiger's eyes. For keeping away bad dreams—or so my grandmother always said."

Cassie managed a small smile for her. "Oh. Thank you." Maybe Melanie's affinity for minerals ran in the family. She didn't bother to tell Aunt Constance what Black John could do to those stones if he tried.

"Bad dreams are a nuisance," old Mrs. Franklin said as Adam and Diana got up to leave. "Of course, good dreams are something else again."

Cassie looked at Adam's grandmother, whose disordered gray hair was coming uncoiled as she happily crunched cookie after cookie. Cassie had never known anybody who liked to eat so much, except Suzan. But there was more to Mrs. Franklin than you'd think at first sight.

"Dreams?" Cassie said.

"Good dreams," Adam's grandmother agreed indistinctly. "For good dreams, you sleep with a moonstone."

Cassie thought about that all the way home.

She and Diana had dinner quietly, just the two of them, since Diana's father was still at his law office. Adam had gone to talk to the rest of the Circle.

"I can't tell them," Cassie had said. "Not tonight—tomorrow, maybe."

"There's no reason you should have to," Adam replied, his voice almost harsh. "You've been through enough. *I'll* tell them—and I'll make them understand. Don't worry, Cassie. They'll stick by you."

Cassie couldn't help but worry. But she put it aside, because she had other things to think about. She'd made a promise to her mother.

She lay in bed reading her grandmother's Book of Shadows. *Her* book of shadows. She was looking for anything about crystals and dreams.

And there it was: *To Cause Dreams. Place a*

moonstone beneath your pillow and all night you will have fair and pleasant dreams which may profit you. She also found a passage about crystals in general. Big crystals were better than little crystals; well, she knew that already. Melanie had said so, and Black John had demonstrated it today beyond question.

She put the book down and went to Diana's desk.

There was a white velvet pouch there, lined with sky-blue silk. Diana had long ago given Cassie permission to open it. Cassie took the pouch to the bed and poured the contents out on a folded-over section of the top sheet. The stones formed a kaleidoscopic array against the white background.

Blue lace agate—Cassie picked up the triangular piece and rubbed its smoothness across her cheek. She saw light yellow citrine— Deborah's stone, good for raising energy. And here was cloudy orange carnelian, which Suzan had once used for raising the passions of the entire football team. Here was translucent green jade, which Melanie used for calm thought, and royal purple amethyst—Laurel's stone, a stone of the heart, Black John had said. There were dozens of others, too: warm amber, light as plastic; dark green bloodstone speckled with red; a wine-colored garnet; the pale green peridot Diana had used to trace the dark energy.

Cassie's fingers sorted through the clinking treasure until she found a moonstone. It was translucent, with a silvery-blue shimmer. She put it on the nightstand by her side of the bed.

Diana came in, fresh from her bath, and watched Cassie putting the stones back into the pouch.

"Find anything in your Book of Shadows?" she asked.

"Nothing specific," Cassie said. She didn't want to explain what she was doing, even to Diana. Later, if it worked. "I'm beginning to think my grandmother didn't mean there was anything specific in the book about Black John," she added. "Maybe she just wanted me to be a good witch, a *knowledgeable* witch. Maybe she'd thought that way I'd be smart enough to beat him."

Diana got in bed and turned off the light. There was no moon; the bay window remained dark. It was peaceful, somehow, with the two of them lying in bed—like a sleepover. It made Cassie think of the old days, when she and Diana had first decided to be adopted sisters.

"We need to find a way to kill him," she said.

A sleepover with a grim and bloodthirsty purpose. Diana was silent for a moment and then said calmly, "Well, we know two things that *can't* kill him—Water and Fire. He drowned the first time when his ship went down, and he burned the second time, when our parents burned the house at Number Thirteen. But he didn't stay dead either time."

Cassie appreciated the "our parents." *Her* mother hadn't been trying to burn anybody, she'd bet.

"He said his spirit didn't need to stay in his body," she said. "I think he can make it go different places. Maybe when he died, he just sent his spirit somewhere else."

"Like into the crystal skull," Diana said. "And it stayed there until we brought it and his body together. Yes. But what can we *use* against him?"

"Earth . . . or Air," Cassie mused. "Though I don't see how Air could kill anybody."

"I don't either. Earth could mean crystals . . . but we don't have a crystal big enough to use against him."

"No," Cassie said. "It sounds like it's the Master Tools or nothing. We've got to find them."

She could feel Diana nodding in the darkness. "But how?"

Cassie reached over and felt for the moonstone. She put it under her pillow.

Maybe it's not the size, but how you use them, she thought. "Good night, Diana," she said, and shut her eyes.

ELEVEN

From the start, this dream was clearer than the others. Or maybe it was Cassie that was clearer; more calm, more aware of what was happening. Saltwater slapped her face; she swallowed some. It was so cold she couldn't feel her hands or feet.

Going down. She was going to drown . . . but not die. With the last of her will she sent her spirit to the place prepared for it . . . to the skull on the island. Some of her power had been left in the skull already; now she herself would go to join it. And someday, when the time was right, when enough of her body diffused through the sea and washed up on the island, she would live again.

Good dreams, I wanted good dreams, Cassie

thought frantically as the water closed over her head.

A shifting . . .

Sunlight blinded her.

"You and Kate may go play in the garden," the kind voice said.

Yes. She'd made it. She was here.

The garden was in back. Cassie turned to the back door.

"Jacinth! What have you forgotten?"

Cassie paused, confused. She had no idea. The tall woman in Puritan dress was looking down at the floor. There, on the clean pine boards, lay the red leather Book of Shadows. Cassie remembered now; it had dropped off her lap when she stood up.

"I'm sorry, Mother." The word came so naturally to her lips. And her eyes had adjusted— but she couldn't figure out where the book was supposed to go. Somewhere special . . . where? Then she saw the loose brick in the fireplace.

"Much better," the tall woman said, as Cassie slid the book into the hole and plugged it up with the brick. "Always remember, Jacinth: we must never grow careless. Not even here in New Salem, where all our neighbors are our own kind. Now run along to the garden."

Kate was already going out the door. In the sunshine outside, Cassie noticed that Kate's hair was just the color of Diana's: not really gold, but a paler color like pure light. Kate's eyes were golden too, like sunshine. She was altogether a golden girl.

"Sky and sea, keep harm from me," she laughed, twirling, looking over the herb bushes to the blue expanse of the ocean beyond the cliff. There was no wall in this time—it hadn't been built yet. Then she darted forward to pick something.

"Just smell this lavender," she said, holding out a bunch to Cassie. "Isn't it sweet?"

But Cassie was hovering by the open door. Two other people had come into the kitchen; Kate's mother and father, she guessed. They were talking in low, urgent voices.

". . . news just came. The ship went down," the man was saying.

There was an exclamation of joy and surprise from Jacinth's mother. "Then he is dead!"

The man shook his head, but Cassie didn't hear the next few words. She was afraid to be caught listening and sent away. ". . . the skull . . ." she heard, and ". . . can never tell . . . come back . . ."

"And this jasmine," Kate was singing. "Isn't it

195

wonderful?" Cassie wanted to tell her to shut up.

Then she heard words that raised the hair on her arms, even in the hot sunshine. ". . . hide them," Kate's mother was saying. "But where?"

That was it. Where, *where*? If this dream had any meaning, it was to tell Cassie this. Kate was trying to put an arm around her waist, to get her to smell the jasmine, but Cassie grabbed her hand to hold her still and strained to listen.

The adults were arguing softly: exclamations of worry and disagreement came to Cassie's ears. "Could we not . . . ?" "No, not there . . ." "But where, then?" "Oh, mercy, my bread is burning!"

And then, soft laughter. "Of course! We should have thought of it earlier."

Where? Fending Kate off, Cassie twisted to try and look into the kitchen.

"Jacinth, what's wrong with you?" Kate cried. "You're not listening to a word I'm saying. Jacinth, look at me!"

Desperately, Cassie stared into the dark kitchen. It was too dark. The dream was fading.

No. She had to hang on to it. She had to see the end. Grandmother, help me, she thought. Help me see . . .

"Jacinth!"

Darker and darker—

Long skirts rustling, moving out of the way. And just a glimpse . . .

"The old hiding place," Jacinth's mother said in a satisfied voice. "Until they are needed again."

Darkness took Cassie.

She woke confused.

At first, she couldn't remember what she'd been looking for in the dream. She remembered the dream, though. Who was Jacinth? An ancestress? One of her great-great-great-great-great-grandmothers, she supposed. And Kate?

Then she remembered her purpose.

The Master Tools. The members of the first coven had hidden them from Black John, because they'd known he might come back. Cassie had gone into the dream to find out where, and she had succeeded.

She'd wondered why Black John had come after her grandmother the night he was released. Not just for the Book of Shadows, she realized now; not just because he'd known her mother and grandmother before. He'd wanted something else from her grandmother. He'd wanted the Master Tools.

But her grandmother hadn't known where

they were. Cassie felt sure that if she had, the old woman would have told *Cassie*. All her grandmother had known was that her own grandmother, Cassie's great-great-grandmother, had told her the fireplace was a good place to hide things. And now, because of the dream, Cassie knew that the loose brick had already been a hiding place in Jacinth's time.

But there had only been one loose brick, and nothing but the Book of Shadows had been stored behind it. Cassie knew that, and she knew that the original coven had been looking for a long-term solution, a place to put the Master Tools "until they were needed" by some future generation. Not just a loose brick, then. Cassie thought about the glimpse of the hearth she'd gotten between the women's skirts in the last second of her dream. The fireplace had been a different shape than it was in modern days.

Cassie lay for a few moments in the velvet darkness. Then she rolled over and gently shook Diana's shoulder.

"Diana, wake up. I know where the Master Tools are."

They woke Adam by throwing pebbles at his window. The three of them went to Number

Twelve armed with a pickax, a sledgehammer, several regular hammers and screwdrivers, a crowbar, and Raj. The German shepherd trotted happily along beside Cassie, looking as if this kind of expedition in the wee hours was just what he liked.

The waning moon was high overhead when they got to Cassie's grandmother's house. Inside, it seemed even colder than outside, and there was a stillness about the place that dampened Cassie's enthusiasm.

"There," she whispered, pointing to the left side of the hearth, where bricks had been added since the time of her dream. "That's where it's different. That's where they must have bricked them up."

"Too bad we don't have a jackhammer," Adam said cheerfully, picking up the crowbar. He seemed undisturbed by the chill and the silence, and in the sickly artificial light of the kitchen his hair gleamed just the color of the garnets in Diana's pouch. Raj sat beside Cassie, his black and tan tail whisking across the kitchen floor. Looking at the two of them made Cassie feel better.

It took a long time. Cassie grazed her knuckles helping to chip the ancient mortar away, using a screwdriver like a chisel. But at last the bricks began to drop onto the cold ashes of the hearth, as one after another was pried out. Each was a different color; some red, some orange, some almost purple-black.

"There's definitely something in here," Adam said, reaching inside the hole they'd made. "But we'll have to get rid of a few more bricks to get it out. . . . There!" He started to reach again, then looked at Cassie. "Why don't you do the honors? It's okay, there's nothing alive inside."

Cassie, who didn't want to encounter a three-hundred-year-old cockroach, nodded at him gratefully. She reached inside and her hand closed on something smooth and cool. It was so heavy she had to use both hands to lift it out.

"A document box," Diana whispered, when Cassie set the thing on the floor in front of the fireplace. It looked like a treasure chest to Cassie, a little treasure chest made of leather and brass. "People used them to store important documents in the 1600s," Diana went on. "We got Black John's papers and things out of one like it. Go on, Cassie, open it."

Cassie looked at her, then at Adam leaning on his pickax, his face decorated with soot. Her fingers trembled as she opened the little box.

What if she'd been wrong? What if it wasn't the Master Tools in here at all, but only some old documents? What if—

Inside the box, looking fresh and untouched as if they'd been buried yesterday, were a diadem, a bracelet, and a garter.

"Oh," breathed Diana.

Cassie knew the diadem that the Circle always used was silver. The one in the box was silver too, but it looked softer, somehow; more heavy and rich, with a deeper luster. Both it and the bracelet looked *crafted*; there was nothing machine-made about them. Every stroke of the bracelet's inscriptions, every intricate twist of the diadem's circlet, showed an artist's hand. The leather of the garter was supple, and instead of one silver buckle, it had seven. It was heavy in Cassie's hand.

Wordlessly, Diana reached out one finger to trace the crescent moon of the diadem.

"The Master Tools," Adam said quietly. "After all that searching, they were right here under our noses."

"So much power," Diana whispered. "I'm surprised they sat here so quietly. I'd have thought they'd be kicking up a psychic disturbance—" She broke off and looked at

Cassie. "Didn't you say something about it being hard to sleep here?"

"Creaks and rattles all night long," Cassie said, and then she met Diana's eyes. "Oh. You mean—you think . . ."

"I don't think it was the house settling," Diana said briefly. "Tools this powerful can make all sorts of strange things happen."

Cassie shut her eyes, disgusted with herself. "How could I have been so stupid? It was so simple. I should have guessed—"

"Everything's always simple in hindsight," Adam said dryly. "*Nobody* guessed where the tools were, not even Black John. Which reminds me: I don't think we'd better tell Faye anything about this."

The two girls looked at him, then Diana nodded slowly. "She told Black John about the amethyst. I'm afraid you're right; she can't be trusted."

"I don't think we should tell *anyone*," Cassie said. "Not yet, anyway. Not until we decide what we're going to do with them. The fewer people who know about this, the safer we are."

"Right," said Adam. He began replacing the bricks in the fireplace. "If we leave everything looking fairly normal, and find a good place to hide that box before morning, no one should ever know we've found them."

"Here." Cassie dropped the garter back in the chest and put the chest into Diana's hands. "Faye's got the other ones; these are yours."

"They belong to the coven leader—"

"The coven leader is a jerk," Cassie said. "These are *yours*, Diana. I found them and I say so."

Adam turned from his brick-replacing, and the three of them looked at each other in the light of the cold, quiet kitchen. They were all dirty; even Diana's beautiful cheekbones bore gray smudges. Cassie was still sore and exhausted from what had been one of the longest and most horrible days in her life. But at that moment she felt a warmth and closeness that swept the pain and fatigue away. They were—connected, all three of them. They were part of each other. And tonight they had won. They had triumphed.

If Diana hadn't forgiven us, where would we be? Cassie wondered, as she looked down at the hearth again.

I'm glad you're the one who has him; I really am, she thought then. Glancing up, she saw that Diana had tears in her eyes, almost as if she knew what Cassie was thinking.

"All right. I'll accept them for now—until it's time to use them," Diana said.

"This is finished," Adam said. They gathered up their tools and left the house.

It was when they were driving back to Adam's that they saw the silhouette beside the road.

"Black John," Cassie hissed, stiffening.

"I don't think so," Adam said, pulling over. "Too little. In fact, I think it's Sean."

It was Sean. He was dressed in jeans and a pajama top and he looked very sleepy.

"What's going on?" he said, his small black eyes darting under heavy lids. "I saw a light over at Cassie's house, and then I saw a car coming out of the driveway . . . I thought you guys were Black John."

"It was brave of you to come out alone," Cassie said, remembering her vow to be kinder to Sean, and pushing away a flicker of uneasiness. Diana and Adam were consulting each other with their eyes, and Sean was looking from their dirty faces to the tools on the jeep's floor, to the hump under Adam's jacket.

"I think we'd better tell him," Diana said. Cassie hesitated—they'd agreed not to tell anyone—but there didn't seem to be any choice.

She nodded slowly, reluctantly.

So Sean climbed in the back and was sworn to secrecy. He was excited about the Master Tools, but Adam wouldn't let him touch them.

"We're going to find somewhere to hide them now," Adam said. "You'd better go back to bed; we'll see you tomorrow."

"Okay." Sean climbed out again. He started to shut the door, then stopped, looking at Cassie. "Oh, hey—you know that stuff about Black John being your father? Well, uh, I just wanted to say—it's okay by me. I mean, you should see *my* father. That's all." He slammed the door and scuttled off.

Cassie felt her throat swell, tears stinging behind her eyes. She'd forgotten about Adam having told them all; she'd have to face the rest of the Circle in the morning. But for now, Sean had made her feel glad and humble.

I've *really* got to be nicer to him in the future, she thought.

They hid the tools in Adam's cellar. "As long as we don't use them nobody should be able to trace them," Diana said. "That's what Melanie and I decided, anyway. But they're dangerous, Adam. It's risky to have them." She looked at him soberly.

"Then let somebody besides you two take a little risk," he said gently. "For once."

Cassie went to bed for the second time that night, tired but triumphant. She put the moonstone back on the dresser; she'd had enough dreams for now. She wondered if she'd ever see Kate again.

"I don't care if her father's Adolph Hitler." Deborah's voice, never soft, rang out clearly from downstairs. Cassie stood just inside the door of Diana's room, hanging on to the doorjamb. "What's it got to do with *Cassie*?"

"We know, Deborah, but hush, can't you?" That was Melanie, a good deal more modulated, but still audible.

"Why don't we just go upstairs an' get her?" Doug said reasonably, and Chris added, "I don't think she's ever comin' down."

"She's probably scared to death of all of you," Laurel scolded, sounding like a cub-scout den mother with a recalcitrant pack on her hands. "Suzan, those muffins are for *her*."

"Are you sure they're oat bran? They taste like dirt," Suzan said calmly.

"You've got to go down sometime," Diana said from behind Cassie.

Cassie nodded, leaning her forehead briefly against the cool wall by the door. The one voice she hadn't heard belonged to the one she was most worried about—Nick. She squared her shoulders, picked up her backpack, and made her legs move. *Now I know how it feels to walk out to face the firing squad,* she thought.

The entire Circle—except Faye—was gathered at the foot of the stairs, gazing up expectantly. Suddenly Cassie felt more like a bride descending the staircase than a prisoner. She was glad she was wearing clean jeans and a cashmere sweater Diana had loaned her, dyed in soft swaths of blue and violet.

"Hi, Cassie," Chris said. "So I hear—yeeouch!" He staggered sideways from Laurel's kick.

"Here, Cassie," Laurel said sweetly. "Have a muffin."

"Don't," Suzan whispered in Cassie's ear.

"I picked these for you," Doug said, thrusting a handful of damp greenery at her. He peered at it doubtfully. "I think they're daisies. They looked better before they died."

"Want to ride to school on my bike?" Deborah said.

"No, she doesn't want to ride to school on

your bike. She's going with me." Nick, who had been sitting on the wooden deacon's bench in the hallway, stood up.

Cassie had been afraid to look him in the face, but now she couldn't help it. He looked cool, unruffled as always, but in the depths of his mahogany eyes there was a warmth that was for her alone. In taking her backpack, his strong, deft fingers squeezed her hand, once.

That was when she knew it was going to be all right.

Cassie looked around at the Club. "You all—I don't know what to say. Thank you." She looked at Adam, who had made them understand. "Thank you."

He shrugged, and only someone who knew him well would have noticed the pain at the edge of his smile. His eyes were dark as storm clouds with some repressed emotion. "Anytime," he said, as Nick started to steer her to the door.

On the way, Cassie glanced back at Doug. "What happened to your *face?*"

"He's always been that ugly," Chris assured her.

"It was the fight," Doug said, touching his black eye with something like pride. "But you should see the other fifty guys," he yelled after her.

"Are we all in trouble for fighting?" Cassie asked Nick, outside.

"Nah—they don't know who started it. They'd have to punish the whole school."

Which, as it turned out, the principal did. The Thanksgiving football game was canceled, and there was a good deal of ill feeling among the students. Cassie just prayed nobody found out where the ill feeling ought to be directed.

"Can we keep things quiet until Thanksgiving vacation next week?" Diana asked at lunch. Cassie and Adam were the only ones who knew exactly why she wanted things kept quiet—so they'd have time to decide how best to use the Master Tools—but the others agreed to try. No one except Doug and Deborah was really interested in more fighting at the moment.

"I'm afraid, though. I'm afraid he'll come after us anyway. He could have the hall monitors pick us up for no reason," Cassie said to Diana afterward.

It didn't happen. A strange peace, a sort of bizarre tranquility, engulfed New Salem High. As if everyone were waiting, but no one knew what for.

*   *   *

"Don't go alone," Diana said. "Wait a minute and I'll go with you."

"I know exactly where the book is," Cassie said. "I won't be in the house more than a minute." She'd been meaning to lend *Le Morte D'Arthur* to Diana for a long time. It was one of her favorite books, and her grandmother had a beautiful copy from 1906. "I can pick up some dried sage for the stuffing while I'm at it," she said.

"No, don't. Don't do anything extra; just come back as quick as you can," Diana said, pushing a strand of damp hair off her forehead with the back of a greasy hand. They'd been having a strenuous but rather interesting time, trying to stuff a Thanksgiving turkey.

"Okay." Cassie drove to Number Twelve. They were late with the turkey; the sun was low in the sky.

Just in and out, Cassie told herself as she hurried through the door. She found the book on a shelf in the library and tucked it under her arm. She wasn't really uneasy—the last week had been so quiet. The Circle had celebrated Suzan's birthday undisturbed two days ago, on the twenty-fourth.

You see, I told you, she thought to Diana as

she came out of the house. Nothing to worry abou—

She saw the car, a gray *BMW*, sitting beside her grandmother's white Rabbit. In that split second, she was already starting to act, to jump back through the doorway, but she never got the chance. A rough hand clapped over her mouth and she was dragged away.

TWELVE

"Get out of here before any of them see us," the voice said tersely. Cassie could smell the acridity of sweat.

Jordan, she was thinking. The one with the gun. The one in the Pistol Club. The other one was Logan, who was on the MIT debate team, and was younger than Jordan—or was he older? Cassie never had been able to keep Portia's brothers straight, even when Portia was telling her about them, back on Cape Cod.

Her mind was working very calmly and clearly. They drove her out of New Salem, onto the mainland, keeping her squashed on the floor of the backseat the whole time. Jordan kept his feet on her and kept something cold and hard pressed against the back of her head. As if I were a dangerous criminal or something, Cassie thought. Good *grief*. What do they think I'm going to do, turn them into toads?

The other pair of feet resting on her was feminine. Portia, Cassie guessed. No, Sally. Portia was too aristocratic to tromp on somebody's legs.

Cassie heard the thudding of the tires as they drove over the bridge to the mainland. After that there were a lot of turns, and then a long ride on a bumpy road. When they finally stopped, it was very quiet.

They were in the middle of a forest. Birch and beech and oak, the native trees of Massachusetts, grew thickly all around. They let Cassie out of the car, and then the guys marched her into the woods. Cassie could hear the lighter footsteps of the girls following. It seemed like a long walk, farther and farther away from the road and any semblance of civilization. As dark fell, they reached a clearing.

Somebody had been here before. Logan's flashlight showed a fire pit, and ropes hanging from a tree. Portia and Sally—Cassie had been right, it *was* Sally—made a fire in the pit, while the guys tied Cassie to the tree. They used a lot more rope than Cassie thought necessary.

And she didn't like the look of that fire.

"Why are you doing this?" she asked Logan as he stepped back from tying her. When she could see their faces she could tell Logan from Jordan—Jordan was the one with shark's eyes.

"Because you're a witch," Logan said briefly.

"That's a *reason?*"

Portia stepped forward. "You lied," she said accusingly. "About the boy on the beach, about everything. All the time, you were a witch yourself."

"I wasn't then," Cassie said, trying to keep her voice steady. "I am now."

"Then you admit it. Well, we're going to do now what we should have done then."

A hard fist of fear clenched in Cassie's stomach, and she looked at the fire again. Jordan was putting something in it, something long and metal.

I'm in trouble, Cassie realized. I am in very, very bad trouble.

She needed help. She knew that, and knew of only one way to call for it. Her only weapon was her power.

All right, she told herself; do what you did to call to Sean. Get ready, stay calm—*now.*

215

Adam, she tried to call to him with her mind. *Adam, it's Cassie. I'm in trouble.* She wished she had the chalcedony rose to hold while she called; Adam had told her it would help make contact with him. But the chalcedony rose was Diana's.

Don't think about that now. Think about Adam. You need to make Adam hear you.

Adam, she called again, putting all her strength behind it. Strange that the ability to push with her mind, to do whatever she did to send the power lancing out, didn't seem to deteriorate with use. Instead, it was like a muscle, getting stronger as she exercised it. *Adam,* she called again, keeping the message simple and clear. *It's Cassie. I need help.*

He'll come, she told herself. He'll find this place somehow; he'll come if I can just stay calm and wait. It was the thought of what might happen *before* Adam came that chilled the blood in her veins.

So here she was, stuck in the middle of nowhere with four witch hunters. And the silence was getting on her nerves.

"The least you can do," she said slowly, speaking to Logan and Sally because she didn't think Jordan or Portia would answer, "is explain

216

yourselves. You've got me out here, and the least you can do is tell me why you hate witches so much. Because I don't understand."

"Are you crazy?" Logan said, as if it should be perfectly obvious. Then, as she continued to stare at him, he said simply, "Because they're evil."

"Logan . . ." Cassie searched his face in the firelight. "We're just like you. We're more—in touch—with nature, that's all. We study it and we celebrate it, and sometimes we can get it to do things for us. But we're not evil. Look," she said, as Logan turned away, "we have our faults like everybody else, but basically we try to be *good*."

"What about Faye Chamberlain?" Sally snapped, joining the conversation suddenly. "Is she good?"

"There's good in Faye," Cassie said, even more slowly. "Diana said that once to me, and it's true. Faye just has to find it. But anyway, you can't judge all of us by one person."

"How about what they did to the entire school for years? You're calling that good? They treated everybody like slaves!"

"That was wrong, I admit it," Cassie said. "But *Diana* didn't do that—if people treated her like a princess, it wasn't her fault. Faye was the one treating people like slaves. Some of the others went along because they didn't *think* about it. And whatever they did, this isn't the way to solve it!"

"Mr. Brunswick is going to solve it," said Portia briefly.

"Mr. Brunswick is a murderer! He is *not* your friend, Portia. He's the one who killed Kori Henderson, Chris and Doug's sister. He killed her because she didn't fit in with his plans. And he killed Mr. Fogle, the old principal, because he wanted to take his place. And," Cassie said, "he killed Jeffrey, Sally! *Yes*. He did it out of spite as far as I can see—or else to drive the witches and the outsiders farther apart. He wants us to hate each other."

"That's ridiculous," Logan said. "Why would he want that?"

"Because," Cassie said, shutting her eyes, knowing it was probably useless, "he is a witch. The bad kind. The only completely bad one I've ever met. And I think he wants us to wipe you out. Or maybe he just wants to take us somewhere else and wipe out the people *there*. I don't *know* what he wants," she said, opening her eyes, "but whatever it is, it isn't good. It isn't something that's going to make you happy."

"Oh, forget this crap. Let's get started," Jordan said.

"No, wait, I want to get something clear." Sally stood in front of Cassie, eye to eye. "You said Brunswick killed Jeffrey—but he couldn't have. He wasn't even in New Salem that night, or when the other murders were committed, either."

"Oh, he was here, he just wasn't up and around," muttered Cassie. She looked at Sally. "He didn't need to be there. He's a witch. He sent out power—dark energy—to do it. Or else maybe he took over somebody's mind and made *them* do it."

Like Faye, Cassie was thinking grimly. When it came right down to it, Faye could have pushed Kori down the steps to break her neck, and could have dislodged a boulder to start a rock slide on Mr. Fogle. She could even have gotten Jeffrey down to the boiler room on some pretext and then strangled him. All it would take would be sneaking up on him from behind and then somehow getting the rope around his neck. The police doctors had said one person could do it.

"What difference does it make, how?" Cassie asked tiredly. "He did it, that's all that matters.

And he *did* do it, Sally, I promise you. He killed Jeffrey."

Sally was staring hard into her eyes, her pugnacious face inches from Cassie's. She shook her head and turned away.

"I'm sorry," Cassie said to the back of her rusty head. "I liked Jeffrey too. I know what you think, that I was trying to steal him or something. But I wasn't. I was just—I was so excited that night at Homecoming. It was the first dance I'd ever been to when guys wanted to dance with me."

"Oh, I'm sure!" Sally snapped without turning around.

"It *was*. It's the truth, Sally," Cassie said passionately. "Back in California I didn't know any guys at all. I was just too shy. I don't even know why they wanted to dance with me at Homecoming. Sally . . ." She gazed at the red-haired girl's tight shoulders helplessly.

Sally turned slowly. "I guess you don't ever look in a mirror," she said, but there was less animosity in her voice.

Cassie blinked away the tears that threatened. "I do, but I don't see anything special," she said. "And I didn't want to steal Jeffrey; I was just so flattered that he asked me. It was a beautiful

220

night, and everything seemed enchanted, and then . . ." She looked from Sally to Logan, blinking again. "You don't know how I felt when I realized he was dead. I would have done anything to catch the person who did it."

Logan took a step toward her, but Portia's voice, sharp as a wasp sting, stopped him. "She's doing it! She's using her witch powers on you, right now. Don't be stupid, Logan."

Cassie looked at her. "Portia, for God's sake . . ."

"Portia's right," Jordan said brutally. "If we listen to her, she'll trick us. She's been a liar from the start." He pulled the metal thing out of the fire.

"What is that?" Cassie asked.

"A cattle brand."

Cassie thought about that, and tried to keep her fragile grip on control. Jordan stepped in front of her, holding the long rod which was red-hot at the end. That didn't surprise Cassie. What surprised her was what he said.

"Where are the Master Tools?" he asked.

Cassie was dumbfounded. "*What?*"

"Mr. Brunswick told us," Portia said, her voice thin and hard. "He told us that they're the source of your power, and that if they're destroyed you lose it all. He wants to destroy them himself and stop you forever."

Cassie had the wild impulse to laugh, but she knew that would only bring more trouble. So *he'd* put them up to this. And he knew she'd found the Master Tools. Right now, he must be expecting her to tell Jordan to save herself. Or maybe he was around here, hoping Cassie would call on him for help.

I won't, Cassie thought. No matter how bad it gets, I won't do it. I don't want to be saved by him.

She looked around the clearing, especially at the shadows that flickered on the edges of the firelight.

"He wants the Master Tools, all right," she said distinctly. "But not to destroy them. He'd use them to destroy *you*, and us, too, if he can't get us to knuckle under."

Jordan looked unsurprised. "You'll tell us in a while," he said. "I expected you to lie at first."

Cassie's entire body tightened as he brought the glowing brand closer to her. I am brave, she thought, trying to calm her heartbeat. I am as strong as I need to be. But when she smelled the hot metal, sheer black fright swept through her.

"Wait! Stop right there, Jurgen and Low-down, or whatever your names are." It was Deborah's voice, angry and filled with elemental savagery. The girl was standing between two trees as if she'd just materialized there this moment. With her tumbled dark hair blending into the black shadows, and her graceful, stalking posture, she might have been some forest goddess come on a mission of vengeance.

Jordan dropped the cattle brand and grabbed his gun, pointing it directly at Deborah.

A new voice spoke quietly from the other side of the grove. "If you move away from Cassie and put the gun down," Adam said in low, precise tones, "we won't have to hurt you." He had appeared just as soundlessly and he looked just as dangerous as Deborah. Cassie thought of the costume he'd worn at Halloween, the stag antlers and autumn leaves of the horned god. Right now she wouldn't have been surprised to see a stag beside him.

There was another slight movement and Cassie saw Diana.

It was as if moonlight had suddenly stepped into the grove. An unearthly aura hung about the girl who stood with fair hair cascading around her like a shining cloak. Tall and slender, she had such an air of command that she might have been the goddess Diana, with the moon and stars at her fingertips. She looked at the outsiders silently with eyes as green as jewels, and then she spoke.

"Get away from my friend," she said.

For an instant Cassie thought they were going to do it on the strength of her authority alone. Jordan's gun wavered. Then it snapped up again, pointing toward Adam, and Logan snatched a burning stick from the fire. He held it close to Cassie's face, as Jordan had held the brand.

"Keep back or we'll hurt *her*," he said.

Adam let out his breath. "We warned you," he said softly.

Cassie was looking into Diana's emerald eyes. She glanced at Logan's burning stick, and then back. She could tell that Diana remembered the candle ceremony.

Fire—so close she could feel its heat on her cheek. The flames changing shape every second, their radiance streaming endlessly upward. There was power in Fire, as Cassie had discovered when Faye had waved a piece of burning paper at her in the old science building. Power there for the taking . . .

This time she took it.

The stick flared up as if someone had dumped

gasoline on it, and Cassie turned her face away, eyes shut against the brilliance. Logan screamed and threw the stick. Jordan's head jerked sideways, he was distracted for an instant—

—and that was all it took. Jordan went down as the Henderson brothers appeared from nowhere, leaping like twin golden flames. The gun fired a shot skyward, and then they were pinning him, one on each arm. Cassie saw Nick surge up from the shadows and grab Logan from behind. Logan struggled, but Adam joined Nick and the fight was over in seconds.

By the time Cassie looked the other way, the outsider girls were taken care of. Sally was on her face, with Deborah kneeling on her back and Melanie standing over them. Portia was flattened against a tree, very still. Two feet from her, Raj was snarling, lips peeled back, hair bristling. Laurel stood just behind him, looking tall and terrible.

"These trees," she said to Portia, "have put up with a lot from your kind. If you try to run you'll end up lost in the middle of them. That's not to mention what the dog might do. If I were you, I wouldn't move a muscle."

Portia didn't.

Diana walked over and cut Cassie's ropes with

a white-handled knife. It took some time.

"Good job," Suzan said from the sidelines.

"Are you all right?" Diana asked Cassie, still with that frightening, unearthly aura about her. Cassie nodded.

"We were already on our way when you called to Adam," Diana said. "Laurel saw their car speeding down Crowhaven Road and Adam felt there was something wrong. He guided us to their car, but it was Raj who tracked you through the woods."

Cassie just nodded gratefully. She couldn't speak.

"Since Cassie's all right, we won't hurt you four," Diana said aloud, then. "But we're going to take *this*"—she picked up Jordan's gun, holding it as if it were a poisonous snake—"and we're going to leave you here. Your car has a few flat tires. You can walk home."

The four outsiders said nothing. Sally, still on the ground, was panting; Logan, with Nick's arm around his throat, was trembling-still; Portia remained frozen against the tree. But it was Jordan who held Cassie's attention. He was staring at Diana with eyes of pure hatred, like a cornered wild dog.

It will never stop, Cassie thought. They'll

hate us even more after this. They'll do something else to us, and we'll do something to them, and it will never stop.

On impulse, she walked over to where Jordan lay sprawled on his back on the forest floor, and she held out a hand to him.

"We don't have to be enemies," she said. "Can't we just end it now?"

Jordan spat on her.

Cassie went still, too surprised to be upset. Nobody had ever spat at her before. She looked in shock at her outstretched hand, then wiped it on her jeans.

What happened next she heard later from Laurel, because she was actually looking down at the time. Nick started toward Jordan instantly, but he was hindered by having to get rid of Logan, and anyway Adam was simply *faster*. He moved faster than the eye could follow, grabbing Jordan by the front of the jacket and hauling him up, then knocking him down again with one lightning-quick blow to the face. Behind Cassie, the bonfire shot up in orange flames ten feet high. Jordan landed on his back, both hands clapped over his nose.

"Get up," Adam said. The flames roared and crackled, sending a shower of sparks floating into the darkness of the woods.

Nick was beside Adam now. His face was emotionless, utterly cool, the old Nick. "Naw, buddy, I think he's had enough," he drawled, taking hold of Adam's arm.

Jordan lifted one hand from his nose, and Cassie saw the blood. "She's a little liar. You'll find out," he yowled in a thick voice, looking from Cassie to Adam.

For a moment Cassie thought Adam was going to hit him again. Then Adam turned away, as if forgetting Jordan existed. He didn't seem to notice Nick's existence either. He took Cassie's hand, the one Jordan had spat on, turned it over, and kissed it.

Cassie thought that somebody had better do something fast.

"We should tie them up," Melanie said, her calm, thoughtful voice pervading the clearing. "Or three of them at least—the fourth can be untying the others while we get away."

"Not too tightly," Diana said, conceding. While Jordan, Logan, and Sally were being tied up, she stuck the white-handled knife in the ground by Portia. "You can cut them free when we leave. Don't try to follow us," she said. Portia didn't look as if she might follow; her eyes were showing white all around.

Diana followed her gaze to the fire, which was still roaring more like a burning oil well than a bonfire, and spoke softly to Cassie. "Can you tone that down a little? I think they're scared enough."

Cassie, who wasn't doing it, mumbled something inarticulate, and hastily went over to check on Sally's bonds.

Sally glanced at her out of the sides of her eyes and spoke without moving her lips. "I was wrong about you."

Cassie looked at her in surprise, but said nothing, leaning over as if to examine Sally's tied wrists.

"You may be right about Brunswick," Sally said, still in almost inaudible tones. "If you are, I feel sorry for you. He's going to do something on the ninth. There's a full moon or something—and that's when he's going to move. He wanted the tools before then."

"Thanks," Cassie whispered and she squeezed Sally's hand behind her back. Then she straightened up as Diana said, "Let's go." As they left, Cassie nudged Adam inconspicuously.

"Are you doing the fire?" she whispered.

"What? Oh." The flames fell, collapsing

suddenly into a normal bonfire. "I guess so," he said.

They walked through the woods, Laurel and Deborah leading them surely among the dark trees, Raj trotting alongside. Cassie spent the entire walk thinking about Nick.

She got in the Armstrong car with him when they came to the road. He drove silently, one arm along the back of the seat. The other cars were in front of them, headlights shining on the lonely road as they made their way back to New Salem.

Cassie was trying to find the right words to say. She'd never had to do anything like this before and she was afraid to do it wrong. She was afraid to hurt Nick.

But there was no way around it. From the instant that Adam had kissed her hand she had *known*. Cassie could like it or hate it, but there was no way to do anything about it.

"Nick . . ." she said, and choked up.

"You don't have to say anything," he said, in his old detached, nothing-hurts-me voice. Cassie could hear the pain underneath it. Then he looked at her, and his tone softened.

"I knew what I was doing when I got into this," he said. "And you never pretended anything else. It's not your fault."

He'd said she didn't have to say anything—but she did. She had to try to explain to him.

"It's not because of Adam," she said softly. "I mean, it's not *for* him, because I know there's no hope. I—*accept* that now, and I'm happy for him and Diana. But I just . . ."

She stopped and shook her head helplessly. "This is going to sound totally stupid, but I can't be with anybody else. Ever. I'm just going to have to . . ." She tried to think of a way to put it, but all she could come up with was a phrase out of one of her grandmother's Victorian etiquette books she'd read one rainy afternoon.

"I'm going to have to live a life of single blessedness," she mumbled.

Nick threw back his head and laughed. Real laughter. Cassie looked at him, embarrassed, but glad that at least he was smiling. His voice was more normal too, as he glanced at her sideways, taking his arm off the back of the seat.

"Oh, you think so?" he said.

"Well, what else am I supposed to do?"

Nick didn't answer, just shook his head slightly, with another little snort of laughter.

"Cassie, I'm glad I met you," he said. "You're—unique. Sometimes I think you belong back in medieval times instead of now. You and Diana and *him*, all three. But, anyway, I'm glad."

Cassie felt more embarrassed, and she didn't understand. "I'm glad I met *you*," she said. "You've been so nice to me—you're such a good guy."

He snorted again. "Most people would disagree," he said. "But I'm not so bad. I'll have to make sure I'm not, or I'll still see you looking at me with those big eyes." He started to fish a cigarette out of the pack in his pocket, then glanced at her sideways and tapped it back.

Cassie smiled. She wished she could hold his hand, but that wouldn't be right. She was going to have to make it alone now.

She leaned back and looked through the windows at the lighted houses slipping by.

THIRTEEN

"It's the Moon of Long Nights," Diana said. "And it's not just full on the ninth. There's an eclipse."

"A total lunar eclipse," said Melanie.

"Is that bad for us?" Cassie asked.

Diana considered. "Well, all witches' powers are strongest in moonlight. And certain spells are best done at the dark of the moon, or at the full moon, or at some other phase. I'm sure that if Black John is going to move on that particular night, an eclipse must be best for whatever he's going to do. And worst for us fighting him."

"Except," Adam said, "if we know he's going to move—and he doesn't know we know it. He won't realize we're prepared."

There were thoughtful nods around the Circle. It was the day after Thanksgiving and everyone who had come to rescue Cassie the day before was gathered at Adam's house. Cassie had told them what had happened in the clearing before they came—except about Jordan asking for the Master Tools. This she'd whispered to Adam and Diana in front of Diana's house last night. Now she looked at the two of them with a question in her eyes.

Adam and Diana both regarded the group unhappily. "Right," Adam said. "I guess we'd better tell them. Since *he* knows, it doesn't really matter, does it?"

"Faye must have found out somehow," Diana said, looking more unhappy than ever. "She went to Black John—"

"No," Cassie said.

Diana looked at her, surprised. "But—"

"Not Faye," Cassie said, grimly and with absolute certainty. "*Sean.*"

Adam cursed softly. Diana stared at him, then at Cassie. Then she whispered, "Oh, my God."

"What about Sean? What did he do?" Deborah demanded. Nick was very alert, his narrow eyes fixed on Cassie.

After a glance at Diana—who nodded and

leaned her head on one hand—Cassie said simply to Deborah, "He told Black John that Adam and Diana and I had found the Master Tools."

"You found—you mean you guys—you mean you really—?" Deborah was sputtering. The others looked speechless with amazement.

"*Cassie* led us to them," Adam said. "They were in the fireplace at Number Twelve. On the way back we ran into Sean, who said he'd seen a light. But you think . . . ?" He looked at Cassie.

Cassie took a deep breath. "I think Black John has been influencing him all along. I think he was the one who stole the hematite from my room. I figured it out last night, when I was trying to get to sleep. I started thinking about who could have told Black John—and I kept getting this flash of Sean the first time I saw him. He was wearing a belt with his name carved on some shiny stone. I used to see him wear it all the time, but now that it's cold and everybody's wearing sweaters, I haven't noticed it. But I'll bet he's been wearing it underneath, and I'll bet he was wearing it that night he came out in his pajama top. And I'll bet that shiny stone is—"

"Hematite," half a dozen bleak voices

chorused, and everyone looked at Melanie.

"Hematite or lodestone," Melanie confirmed. "Yes, it is; I've seen that belt too. How incredibly stupid of us. It never even occurred to me."

Nick leaned forward. "So you think Faye *wasn't* the one who told Black John we were wearing amethysts as protection? You think Sean did that?"

Cassie looked at the hard line of his mouth. "It wasn't his fault, Nick. If Black John got into his mind—well, I know how I felt when he was trying to get into *my* mind. Sean wouldn't have been able to resist. In fact, *we* saw that he couldn't resist, at the assembly when he volunteered to be a hall monitor. I had to yell at him to break the trance."

"Sean . . . God!" Laurel said, settling back. "It's just too awful."

"I'm afraid it's worse," Cassie said. She stared down at Mrs. Franklin's coffee table, pressing one hand flat against it. She didn't know how to say this next. "You guys, I think . . . I think Black John used Sean to commit the murders."

There was a deafening silence. Even Diana looked too horrified to support Cassie. But Adam looked into her eyes and then slowly, shutting his own eyes, nodded.

"Yes," he said.

"Oh, *no*," said Suzan.

"I think"—Cassie swallowed—"that he could have written a note to Kori the night before, asking her to meet him in front of school. She wouldn't have suspected him; she'd have just thought it was Circle business. He could have come up behind her, and—"

"I'll kill him!" Doug shouted, jumping up. Nick and Deborah grabbed him, but by then Chris was shouting too, lunging for the door. Adam and Melanie wrestled him to the ground.

"It wasn't *him*; it wasn't Sean," Cassie shouted. "Listen to me, you guys! It was Black John; *he's* the one who killed Kori. If I'm right, Sean probably doesn't even remember it! He was just a—a *container* for the dark energy to use."

"God," Laurel said. "God—remember the skull ceremony in Diana's garage? The time the second bunch of dark energy was released? Sean and Faye started fighting, the candle went out, and the dark energy escaped. Sean said Faye started it, and we all believed him. But Faye said Sean was trying to break the circle. What if she was right?"

"I'll bet she *was* right," Cassie said. "Black

John's been with us all the time. Whatever Sean saw, he saw. And when enough dark energy was released from the skull—which Black John *arranged* to happen whenever he could—then it worked with Sean to commit the murders."

"It would have been easy to get Mr. Fogle over to Devil's Cove, too," Suzan said. "Sean could have pretended he had something bad to tell about somebody else in the Club. I used to do that all the time; tell the principal things about—" She glanced at Diana. "Well—that was in the old days. Anyway, Sean could have asked Fogle to meet him under the rocks and then—*foom*." She made a pushing gesture. "Good-bye, Mr. Fogle."

"Can we let you up now?" Adam asked Chris, and "Can we trust you to act sensible?" Deborah asked Doug.

There were incoherent snarls from the Henderson brothers, and when they were released they sat up with flushed faces and blue-green eyes as bright as gas flames.

"We're gonna get that bastard," Doug said quietly.

"If it's the last thing we do," said Chris, equally quiet. Cassie hoped they meant Black John.

"But what about Jeffrey?" Diana asked Cassie.

Cassie shrugged. "I don't know how Sean could have gotten him down to the boiler room—"

"By saying *you* were down there, maybe," Laurel said.

"—but if he did, he could have just come up behind him and strangled him with the rope—no, Sean's too short. Oh, I don't know how he could have done it—"

"By getting Lovejoy to sit down or lean over," Nick said, his voice crisp and low. "That's what I'd have done, anyway, if I were trying to strangle somebody that much taller. And look, if Sean had that dark energy *inside* him somehow, he could have had outrageous strength. He must have had, to be able to put the noose around Lovejoy's neck and haul him up over that pipe afterward."

Cassie felt sick. "It's true—I didn't see either Sean or Jeffrey at the dance for a while before the murder. Then all of a sudden Sean appeared on the dance floor, coming toward me. So I ran to the boiler room . . . and found Jeffrey."

"I think we need to talk to Sean," said Diana.

"No," Adam said, with surprising vehemence. "That's just what we shouldn't do. If we talk to him now, Black John will realize we know. But if we don't say anything, if we play along with Sean and pretend we *don't* know, we can feed him disinformation. Tell him things that aren't true, for him to pass along to Black John."

"Like tell him we don't know when Black John is going to move," Deborah said, her dark eyes beginning to snap. "Tell him we're terrified of Black John—we don't know how to use the Master Tools—we're unprepared . . ."

"Or that we're all fighting among ourselves," suggested Laurel. "We can't agree on anything. We're deadlocked."

"Right! And then that night we'll actually be ready for him. When's the eclipse, Melanie?" Adam said.

"Around six forty in the evening. That's what I'd say we have to look out for. The moon in shadow."

"The moon in shadow," Cassie repeated softly. "I think I can understand why he would choose that time." He's a shadow himself, she thought.

"And until then all we have to do is pretend to be completely disorganized, terrified, and argumentative," said Melanie.

"Shouldn't be too hard," Suzan said, raising an eyebrow.

"There's somebody I think we *should* talk to," Cassie said, "without giving away any of our secrets. I think one of us should talk to Faye."

"And I think you're elected," Nick said. "I can't think of anybody better for the job." He winked at Cassie, but it was a grim wink.

"We need you."

"I'm sure," Faye said lazily, examining herself in the mirror. She was trying her hair in different ways: twisted back, on top of her head, at the nape of her neck. Cassie hadn't been in Faye's bedroom since the night Faye had set a ring of red stones around the crystal skull and released the dark energy that had eventually killed Jeffrey. The room was as opulent and luxurious as ever: the wallpaper patterned with lush jungle orchids, the bed piled with cushions, the stereo system packed with expensive extras. Faye's vampire kittens once again twined sinuously around Cassie's ankles.

But there was a different atmosphere here than before. The red candles were gone from the dresser tops; in their place were stacks of paperwork. On the bedspread along with the cordless phone was a beeper. An appointment book was sitting in front of the mirror, and the clothes strewn carelessly about were of the sultry office-girl kind Faye had taken to wearing.

The room felt—pressured. Type-A lifestyle. More like Portia than Faye.

"I suppose you know that Portia Bainbridge and Sally had me kidnapped two days ago," Cassie said.

Faye shot her an amused glance in the mirror. "And I'm sure you know you only had to open your pretty little mouth and yell, and Daddy would have been right there to help."

Cassie tried not to look as sick as that made her feel. "I don't want his help," she said, swallowing.

Faye shrugged. "Maybe later."

"*No*, Faye. Not later. I don't ever want to see him again. But if you know about me being kidnapped, you must know what they were after. We've found the Master Tools." Cassie looked at the strange opposite-Faye image in the mirror, and then turned to look the real Faye in the eyes. "They belong to you," she said distinctly. "You're leader of the coven. But the coven is going to fight . . . Black John."

"You can't even say it, can you? It's not so hard. Daddy. Father. Pops. Whatever you want to call him, I'm sure he won't mind—"

"Will you listen to me, Faye!" Cassie almost shouted. "You're sitting here being fatuous—"

"And she knows big words, too!"

"—while something *serious* is going on! Something deadly serious. He is going to *kill* people. That's all he is, Faye, hatred and the desire to kill. I know it; I can feel it in him. And he's taking *you* for a ride."

Faye's golden eyes narrowed. She looked less amused.

"I've known you for a while now, Faye, and there've been plenty of times when I've hated you. But I never thought I'd see you become somebody's *stenographer*. You used to make up your own mind about things and you didn't kiss up to anybody. Do you remember how you once asked me if I wanted my epitaph to be 'Here lies Cassie. She was . . . nice'? Well, do you want yours to be 'Here lies Faye. She was a good secretary'?"

One of Faye's hands, with its long fingernails—mauve these days, instead of scarlet—was clenched on the dresser. Her jaw was set, and she was staring hard into her own golden eyes in the mirror.

Cassie's pulse quickened. "When I looked at you I used to see a lion—a sort of black and gold

243

lion. Now I see"—she glanced down at her feet—"a kitten. Some rich guy's kitten."

She waited tensely. Maybe . . . just maybe . . . Maybe the bond forged during the candle ceremony would be strong enough, maybe Faye had enough pride, enough independence . . .

Faye's eyes met hers in the mirror. Then Faye shook her head. Her face was closed, her mouth tight.

"I think you know the way out," she said.

The kittens tangled around Cassie's feet as she turned, and she felt the razor-sharp nick of claws.

No, she told them with her mind, and she felt the kittens freeze, ears back. She picked them up, one in each hand, and tossed them onto Faye's bed.

Then she left.

"We have to give her until the ninth," Diana said. "Maybe she'll change her mind."

"'Maybe later,'" Cassie quoted, but there wasn't much hope in her voice.

"We'll wait until the ninth for Sean, too," Adam said.

They made it through the next seven school days without trouble—except among themselves.

At New Salem High, the members of the Club only spoke to each other in public to argue. Laurel's birthday on the first and Sean's birthday on the third of December went uncelebrated, because, according to a distraught Diana, none of them could get along long enough to plan a party. Cassie saw the looks and heard the whispers and knew that the plan was working. She concentrated on being as much like the old Cassie as possible—shy, tongue-tied, easily frightened or embarrassed. The role was uncomfortable, like some old skin she'd outgrown, and she itched to get rid of it. But for the time they were fooling Sean. They were even fooling Faye.

"I hear you and Nick have broken up," Faye said in the hall one day. The hooded golden eyes were warm and pleased.

Cassie flushed, looking away.

"And the Club isn't much of a club without me, from what I see these days," Faye went on, practically purring.

Cassie squirmed.

"I may join you sometime—maybe for the next full-moon celebration. If you're having one, that is."

Cassie shrugged.

Faye looked smug. "We could have a *wicked* time," she said. "Think about it."

As Faye walked away Cassie saw Sally Waltman at her post as hall monitor. She edged up as inconspicuously as possible.

"We're ready for the ninth, like you told us," Cassie said softly. "But can you do one more thing for us?"

Sally looked uneasy. "He's got everybody watching everybody. Nobody's safe—"

"I know, but when the ninth comes, will you tell us if he does anything unusual? If it looks like he's moving? Please, Sally. Everything I told you about him is true."

"All right," Sally said, casting a hunted glance around. "Now just *go*, will you? I'll try to get a message to you if I hear anything."

Cassie nodded and hurried away.

The ninth dawned gray and windy, the sort of day that normally made Cassie want to curl up in front of a fire. Instead, she put on extra-warm clothes: a thick sweater, gloves, a parka. She had no idea what they might be facing today, but she wanted to be dressed for action. In her backpack, along with her school notebooks, she put her Book of Shadows.

She was walking out of French class when Sally intercepted her.

"Come with me, please," the rusty-haired girl said in crisp hall-monitor accents, and Cassie followed her into the empty nurse's office next door. Sally immediately dropped the officious tone.

"If I get caught with you, it's all over," she said rapidly in a harsh whisper, her eyes on the frosted-glass window in the door. "But here it is: I just overheard Brunswick talking with your friend Faye. Maybe *you'll* understand what it was about, because I sure don't. They were discussing something about arranging an accident on the bridge—it sounded like they were taking an empty school bus over there, and a car, or maybe it was a couple of cars. He said 'They only have to burn for an hour or so; by then the water will have risen far enough.' Does that mean anything to you?"

"An accident would block the bridge to the mainland," Cassie said slowly.

"Sure, but why?" Sally asked impatiently.

"I don't know. I'm going to find out. Sally, if I need to see you again, will you be in the cafeteria at lunch?"

"Yes, but you can't talk to me there. Portia's

been looking at me strangely ever since that night in the clearing—I think she's suspicious. Her brothers went away mad, and she didn't believe a word you said about Brunswick. If she catches me with you, I'm dead."

"You may be dead if I *don't* talk with you," Cassie said. "Go on, get out of here, I'll leave in a minute."

Cassie reached the old science building at a run. Waiting on the second floor was the rest of the Club—minus Faye and Sean, who hadn't been informed of the meeting. The plan had been to nab Sean right after lunch, even if they hadn't learned anything about Black John's plans by then.

"But we do know something," Cassie said breathlessly, sitting down on a crate. "Listen." She told them what Sally had said.

"Well, that explains it," Deborah put in when Cassie finished. "I just saw him and Faye walk out of the building, and the secretary said they'd be gone all afternoon. So they're going out to wreck a school bus. Cool."

"But *why?*" Cassie said. "I mean, it looks like he wants to block the bridge, but what's the point?"

It was Adam who answered. He'd been sitting

by Doug, with one of the earphones from Doug's Walkman pressed to his ear.

"The point," he said, "is to keep everybody on the island. There's just been an update on the news—anybody remember that hurricane they were talking about the last couple days? The one that they were afraid was going to hit Florida, but then it turned north while it was still out in the Atlantic?"

There was head-shaking around the group—most of them hadn't been too interested in the news lately—but Melanie said, "I thought they downgraded that to a tropical storm."

"Yeah, they figured it was just going to dissipate out in the ocean. Look, I know a little about hurricanes. This one isn't supposed to be a threat, because they're assuming it's going to turn northeast at Cape Hatteras. That's what hurricanes usually do when they hit the low-pressure trough around there. But we all know what happens when they *don't*." He looked around the group grimly, and this time there were nods from everyone but Cassie.

"When they don't turn at Cape Hatteras, they come barreling straight up here," Adam said to her, then. "Like the one in 1938, and the one a few years ago . . . and the one in 1976."

The silence was absolute. Cassie glanced from side to side at the faces in the dim room.

"God," she whispered, feeling dizzy.

"Yes," said Adam. "Winds a hundred and fifty miles an hour, and *walls* of water, forty feet high. Now, they're still *saying* this storm is going to turn—they just mentioned on the radio that it's supposed to stay well off the Atlantic seaboard. But"—he looked around again, deliberately—"anybody want to take bets?"

Laurel jumped up. "We've got to stop Black John. If that bridge is blocked, everybody on the island is in danger."

"Too late," Deborah said briefly. "He's already gone. Remember? I saw him leave ten minutes ago."

"And everybody's not just in danger, everybody's *dead*," Melanie said. "That storm a couple years ago just nicked New Salem, but this one could wipe us out."

Cassie looked at Adam. "How fast is it coming?"

"I don't know. Could be fifty miles an hour, could be seventy. If it doesn't turn at Cape Hatteras, they'll issue a hurricane warning—but it'll be too late by then, especially if the bridge is blocked. It could get to us in maybe seven, eight hours. More or less."

"Around the time of the eclipse?" Cassie asked.

"Maybe. Maybe a little later."

"But before it hits us, it'll hit Cape Cod and Boston," Diana whispered. "It will *kill* people there." She looked stunned and dazed at the idea.

"Then there's only one thing to do," Cassie said. "We've got to stop it before it hits land at all. We've got to make it dissipate, or turn back out to the ocean, or whatever. Or we've got to make *him* do it. And before that we've got to warn people on our own—tell them to do whatever you do in a hurricane—"

"Evacuate," Adam said dryly, "which may not be possible, even in boats. Listen to that wind." He paused and Cassie heard not only the wind but a pattering on the boarded-up windows. Rain.

"If they can't get out, they'll have to dig in," Chris said. "Anybody up for a hurricane party?"

"It's not funny," Nick said sharply, and Cassie said, "All right, then—tell people to do *that*. Do whatever they can. And we'd better get back to Crowhaven Road—"

"With Sean," Adam cut in swiftly. "I'll get

him and meet everybody at my house. Let's do it, people."

They left their uneaten lunches—except Suzan, who snagged hers and ran after the others—and headed for the school.

FOURTEEN

"So you have to go now," Cassie said, trying to get her breath, speaking not only to Sally but to everyone in the cafeteria. "Forget school, forget everything. Leave. Get out if you can, and if you can't—well, do whatever you can to protect yourselves." She stopped. "Look, it's *true*. Sally, tell them."

The rusty-haired girl had been staring at Cassie, eyes wary, poised on her chair as if to bolt from this social pariah. Now she stared at Cassie another moment, then nodded once, as if to herself. Taking a deep breath, she stood.

"Okay, you heard it," she said in clear, strident tones that carried through the room. "We're going to have a hurricane. Everybody tell somebody, and tell them to tell somebody else. Come on, get moving."

A boy stood up. "I saw on TV last night that the storm isn't coming anywhere near us. How does she know—"

"She's a witch, isn't she?" Sally yelled back in her raucous voice. "You telling me witches don't know these things? They know more about nature than you ever will! Now come on!"

"Sally, have you lost your *mind*?" The thin angry voice came from the door of the back room, where Portia was standing in front of a group of students with badges, her face chalky with fury. "You're a hall monitor—"

"Not anymore! I said move, you guys!"

"This is completely against regulations! I'm going to tell Mr. Brunswick—"

"You do that, cupcake," Sally shouted back. "*If* you can find him! Now for the last time, people, get moving! Who are you going to listen to, her or me?"

The hall monitors behind Portia hesitated for an instant, then, as a group, they surged forward to obey Sally. Portia stumbled back as they pushed around her, leaving her the sole inhabitant of the room. Cassie's last glimpse of her showed her standing there, rigid, furious, and utterly alone.

Sally began to shout more instructions to the cafeteria workers, and Cassie turned to go. But as Cassie reached the door, each of the girls paused a moment, and looked back at the other across the room.

"You going to be okay?" Sally said. Cassie knew the "you" didn't just mean Cassie. It meant the whole Circle.

"Yes."

"Okay. Good luck."

"You too. Good-bye, Sally."

It wasn't much of a brilliant cultural exchange, Cassie thought, running toward the parking lot to meet Diana. But it was a truce, witch with outsider. More than a truce.

And now, she thought, I've got to put them out of my mind—all the outsiders. Sally will take care of her people; we have to take care of ours.

It was raining hard now, and it seemed to get worse as she and Diana drove toward Crowhaven Road. Gusts of wind swayed Diana's car as they pulled into Adam's driveway.

Right behind them, Adam's jeep was pulling in. "They've got Sean," Cassie said, twisting to

255

look. She and Diana hurried to help.

Nick and Doug were holding the smaller boy in the backseat. They marched him to the door the way Portia's brothers had marched Cassie. It seemed a little incongruous; Sean was *so* small—but then Cassie looked into those shiny, darting black eyes.

"You'd better get the hematite off him quick," she said.

Nick pulled Sean's sweater up—and there it was, the engraved belt Cassie had seen that first week of school. Adam unbuckled it and threw it on the floor, where it lay like a dead snake. "Where's the other piece?" he asked Sean roughly.

Sean just fought to get free, panting, his eyes wild. It took all three of the guys to hold him, and if Chris, Deborah, and Laurel hadn't arrived at that moment, he might actually have gotten away. Working together, the boys and Deborah managed to strip off his sweater and shirt. Underneath, where the other members of the Circle had been wearing amethysts, Sean was wearing a small leather pouch. Adam shook it gingerly and Cassie's piece of hematite fell out.

"Thief!" Deborah said, shaking a fist in Sean's face. Sean stared at her blankly, still panting, terrified.

"He probably didn't even know he had it," Melanie intervened. "He's been under Black John's influence from the beginning. Somebody take that hematite out and bury it. Laurel, is the herbal bath ready?"

"Ready!" came Laurel's shout from the downstairs bathroom, over the sound of running water. "Get him in here."

The Circle had been planning this purification ritual ever since they'd found out about Sean, and everyone knew his or her part. The boys dragged Sean into the bathroom while Laurel stood just outside the door. "I don't care if his clothes are off or on," Cassie heard her calling. "Just get him in the tub."

Deborah scooped up the hematite in a dustpan and went to bury it, and Diana rapidly completed an herbal charm she took from her backpack. She charged the canvas pouch of herbs with Earth, Water, Air, and Fire by sprinkling salt on it, flicking water from a glass on it, breathing on it, and passing it over a lit candle which had been sitting ready on the coffee table.

"Okay, it's done," she said. "Melanie, what about you?"

Melanie looked up from laying a ring of

white stones on the floor. "I'm done too. By the time we're finished with Sean, he'll be so pure we won't know him anymore."

Cassie wanted to look something up in her Book of Shadows, but there was another priority first.

"We have to warn the parents around here," she said, "the ones who're at home, who don't work. Is somebody doing that?"

"I'll go to my house," Chris said. "Both of my parents are home."

"My mom works," Deborah said.

"That just leaves Faye's mom," said Diana.

"I'll go tell her," Suzan offered, surprising Cassie. "She knows me, she might take it best from me."

"And the crones," Cassie said. "I mean," she amended quickly, "Adam's grandmother and Granny Quincey and Aunt Constance."

"They're at my house; they came over this morning," Melanie said. "Something to do with your mom, I think, Cassie. But I can't leave this circle."

"I'll go," Cassie said.

Diana flashed a smile at her. "I think crones is a good name for them," she said. "It's what they are, and I think Granny Quincey, anyway, would be proud to be crone to our coven."

So would my grandma, I bet, Cassie thought, and she plunged outside again.

There was a strange smell out here, a smell like low tide, like crawling and decaying things. Cassie ran to the edge of the cliff, taking the back route along the bluff to Melanie's house, and she saw that the ocean was dark and wild. The water was neither blue nor green nor gray, but a sludgy, oily color that seemed to be a mixture of all three. Specks of foam were flying on the wind, and there was white froth everywhere.

Above, the clouds took on fantastic shapes, boiling and changing as if molded by unseen hands. The rain drove into Cassie's face. It was a savage and awe-inspiring scene.

No one answered her knock at the door of Number Four. Cassie wasn't sure anybody inside could hear it over the wind and rain. "Aunt Constance?" she shouted, opening the door and peering inside. "Hello?"

She started toward the room that had been given to her mother, and then stopped, turned back guiltily, and wiped her sandy, muddy Reeboks on the mat. Even so, she dripped water on the spotless, mirror-polished hardwood floor as she hurried to the bedroom. The door was barely ajar, and a strange brightness flickered inside.

"Hello? . . . Oh, my God!" Cassie poked her head around the door and froze. The room was lit entirely by dozens of white candles. Around the bed were three figures, three women whose appearance was so strange and fantastic that for a moment Cassie didn't recognize them.

One was tall and thin, another was short and plump, and the third was tiny and doll-like. They all had long hair: the tall one's was black and thick, longer than Diana's, the plump one's was silvery-gray and untidy, waving down past her shoulders, and the tiny one's was gauzy and white like floating wisps of seafoam. And they were naked.

Cassie's eyes were popping. "Great-aunt Constance?" she gasped to the one with long black hair.

"Who did you expect?" Melanie's aunt said sharply, her meticulously tweezed eyebrows drawing together. "Lady Godiva? Now go away, child, we're busy."

"Don't be unkind to her," said the plump woman, whom Cassie was now able to identify as Adam's grandmother. She smiled at Cassie, entirely unself-conscious.

"We're trying something to help your mother, dear," the tiny figure, Laurel's Granny Quincey, added. "It's a sky-clad ritual, you see; that's why we're naked. Constance had her doubts, but we convinced her."

"And we need to get on with it," Great-aunt Constance said, gesturing with the wooden cup she was holding. Granny Quincey was holding a bunch of herbs, and Adam's grandmother, a silver bell. Cassie looked at the bed, where her mother lay as motionless as ever. Something about the light in the room made that sleeping face look different, just as it made the three women look different.

"But there's a hurricane coming," Cassie said. "That's why I'm here; I came to warn you."

The women exchanged glances. "Well, if there is, there's no help for it," Adam's grandmother sighed.

"But—"

"Your mother can't be moved, dear," Granny Quincey said firmly. "So you go along and do what you have to, and we'll try to protect her here."

"We're going to fight Black John," Cassie said. The simple statement seemed to hang in the air after she'd said it, and the three old women looked at each other again.

Great-aunt Constance opened her mouth, frowning, but Granny Quincey interrupted her. "There's no one else *to* do it, Constance. They have to fight."

"Then be careful. You tell Melanie—and all of them—to be careful," Aunt Constance said.

"And you stick together. As long as you stick together you'll have a chance," said Adam's grandmother.

And that was that. The women turned back to the bed. Cassie stood for one more moment looking at the candles—so white, with their flames even whiter, a golden white like Diana's hair—and at the myriad ghostly shadows on the ceiling and walls. Then she left. As she quietly shut the door, all the candle flames danced wildly, and she had a last glimpse of the three women in the room, arms raised, beginning a kind of dance too. The silver bell chimed softly.

She hadn't noticed the wind inside the room, but now she did. Everything outside that door seemed colder and noisier, and the dim light coming in through the windows looked gray and wintry. Cassie had an impulse to go back into the golden room and hide there, but she knew she couldn't.

She walked back to Adam's house, Number Nine, with the wind pushing her all the way.

She was the last one back. The Circle was in Adam's living room, sitting around Sean, who was sitting within the circle of quartz crystals. Sean's face was very pink and scrubbed-looking, his hair was wet and spiky, and he was wearing clothes too big for him. Adam's, Cassie guessed. Around his neck was the canvas pouch full of herbs Diana had prepared. He looked dazed and terrified, but he didn't seem to be trying to get away.

"Were they there? Did you find them?" Diana asked Cassie.

Cassie nodded. She didn't quite want to tell Diana *how* she had found them. She didn't know how Melanie and Adam and Laurel would feel about their elderly relatives dancing naked around a sickroom. They might think there was something wrong with it; they might not understand about the golden light.

"They said they'd stay where they were," she said. "Granny Quincey said my mom couldn't be moved, and that they were trying to help her. They said we should be careful, and

Adam's grandmother told us to stick together."

"Good advice," Adam said, looking at Sean. "And that's just about the point we've gotten to, here. Are we going to stick together or not?"

"We tried asking him about the murders," Laurel informed Cassie in a low voice, "but he doesn't remember anything—doesn't know what we're talking about. We had to convince him that it wasn't a joke. He believes us now, but he's scared to death."

"So here's the choice, Sean," Adam was saying. "You can stand with us, or you can spend the rest of the day locked in the cellar where you can't make trouble."

"Or," Diana said softly, "you can go to *him*, to Black John. It's his right," she added quickly, as some of the others began to protest. "He has to make the decision."

Sean's frightened eyes roved all around the room. Cassie felt sorry for him, sitting surrounded, with everyone looking at him. When he spoke, his voice was squeaky but definitive. "I'll stand with you guys."

"Good boy," Laurel said approvingly, and Deborah thumped him on the back so hard he nearly fell over. The Hendersons said nothing, simply looked at him out of their strange blue-green eyes, and Cassie had the feeling they might never forgive him for what had happened to Kori, even if it hadn't been his fault. But at least for now, the Circle stood together.

Except . . .

Cassie looked at Adam, and they both looked at Diana. Diana nodded.

"Now's the time," she said. "This is Faye's last chance—let's hope she takes it."

Cassie didn't have much hope, but she picked up the cordless phone lying on a pile of unfolded laundry on the couch. "What's her beeper number?"

Diana unfolded a scrap of paper and read it off. "After it rings, press pound and then dial Adam's number," she instructed.

Cassie did and turned off the phone. She waited. Nothing happened.

"We should give her a while to get to a phone," Diana said.

They all waited. Rain beat at the windows, and the wind howled in the chimney.

"Isn't there anything we should do? Like—I don't know, nail boards over the windows or something?" Cassie asked.

"Normally, yeah. We'd put up storm shutters,

lash everything down, all that stuff," Adam said. "But if this one hits us, I think we're history, so there's not much point."

They waited.

"Try her again," Diana said, and Cassie did.

"Her mom hadn't seen her since this morning," Suzan said. "I wonder where she and Black John are?"

Cassie wondered too. Wherever they were, Faye wasn't answering her beeper.

"I think," Cassie said at last, "that we're out one coven leader. And—well, I wanted to look this up in my Book of Shadows first, but Melanie, doesn't it say somewhere that in an emergency you can elect a new leader?"

Melanie smiled faintly, then nodded, as if she knew what Cassie had in mind. "In a crisis," she said. "If the remaining coven all agrees, a new leader can be elected."

There was a shifting around the Circle, people straightening up and looking interested. "Oh," said Laurel, "that's a *good* idea."

"Especially since we've got the Master Tools," Adam said.

"Let's do it," said Deborah.

Cassie was excited. She'd taken an oath while watching Faye draw that circle at the crossroads, and now she was going to see her oath fulfilled. She'd promised that Faye wouldn't be leader forever, and in a few minutes Faye *wouldn't* be.

She opened her mouth joyfully to say, "I nominate Diana," but before she could speak she heard Diana's voice.

"I nominate Cassie," Diana said clearly.

Cassie simply stared at her, amazed. When she got her breath back she said, "You're joking."

"No," Diana said. Then she turned, speaking to the rest of the Circle, speaking formally. "Cassie," she said, "has shown the most power of any of us, including Faye. She can call on the elements—we've seen her call on Fire. She can communicate over long distances. She's had true dreams, and she was the one who led us to the Master Tools. Her grandmother told her that her family has always had the clearest sight and the most power. And she's strong, stronger than I am for this kind of fight. I nominate Cassie."

Cassie was stunned, but the others were nodding.

"She's pretty tough," Deborah said, "even if she doesn't look like it."

"She got that dog off me," said Chris, sticking out his foot and examining it.

"She's smart, too," said Laurel proudly. Aside from Diana, Laurel had been Cassie's first friend in the Circle. "She thinks of things most people wouldn't think of."

"She has ideas," Suzan agreed, nodding her strawberry-blond head sagely.

"I like her," Sean ventured hesitantly, from his place in the ring of white stones. "She's nice to me."

"She's a natural," Doug said, grinning his wild grin.

Nick just said, *"Yes."*

Cassie realized they were serious. "I'm also Black John's . . . " She stopped and tried again. "The fact that Black John is my . . . " She still couldn't say the word.

"I think that may actually work *for* us," Melanie said, looking at Cassie with thoughtful gray eyes. "If he doesn't really want to hurt you it might handicap him—a little."

Everyone was still nodding. Cassie swallowed and gazed around the Circle. It didn't seem to have occurred to anyone that she might just be too *scared* to do it, to lead the fight against Black John. In her own heart, she knew she didn't want to face him again—that she wasn't ready. She didn't know if she'd ever be ready.

But they were all looking at her: Diana with earnest faith; Deborah and the Hendersons with innocent confidence. Even Nick and Melanie were nodding, urging her.

Cassie looked at Adam.

His blue-gray eyes were something like the ocean outside—murky and full of turmoil. "You can do it," he said tersely, answering her unspoken question. "And I think it's best for the coven. I don't know if it's best for *you*."

Cassie let out her breath.

They believed in her. She couldn't let them down.

"If everybody agrees," she said, scarcely knowing her own voice.

"We'll do it the easy way," Melanie said. "All in favor of Cassie as leader, raise your hand."

Every hand was raised.

Diana jumped up. "I'll get the things," she said. She and Adam headed for the cellar and returned a few minutes later with the brass and leather document box. Everyone leaned forward to look as she opened it, and there was a soft hiss of amazement around the Circle.

"They're beautiful," Suzan said, touching the silver diadem with one perfectly manicured nail.

"Yes," said Diana, unzipping her backpack. "Here, Cassie, put this on." It was the white shift Diana wore at meetings.

Cassie felt heat stealing into her face. She *couldn't* wear that. She would look . . .

"Don't worry, you won't be cold," Diana said, and smiled.

"But—you're taller than me. It'll be too long—"

"I hemmed it," Diana said. And then, in the silence that followed, she said gently, "Take it, Cassie."

Slowly, Cassie took it. She went into the bathroom, still slightly steamy now, where the boys had washed Sean, and she put on the raw-silk shift. It fit perfectly.

Diana had this planned, she realized.

She was embarrassed to walk back out, but she told herself this was no time to be worried about how much skin she was showing. Chris and Doug whistled as she rejoined the group.

"Shut up, this is serious," Laurel said.

"She might as well stand here, in the circle of white stones," Melanie said. "Get out, Sean."

Sean, looking relieved, stepped out. Cassie stepped in.

Silence fell.

"I adjure thee to work for the good of the Circle, to harm none, to be faithful to all. By Water, by Fire, by Earth, and by Air, lead us peacefully and with good will," Diana said. Cassie realized she was getting the part of the ceremony that Faye had missed when Faye had become leader.

"Look—this is only temporary, isn't it—?" she began.

"Sh," said Laurel, kneeling. Cassie felt something soft being fastened just above her right knee. She looked down to see Laurel buckling the green leather garter.

Coolness encircled Cassie's upper arm, and she turned to see Melanie clasping the silver bracelet there. It was surprisingly heavy; Cassie knew she'd feel the weight whenever she moved that arm.

"Look at me," Diana said. Cassie did. Between her two hands Diana was holding the diadem of delicate twisted silver, with the crescent moon on top. Cassie felt it settle into her hair, lightly but firmly. And then, all over her body, from the silver of the garter buckles,

271

to the silver of the bracelet, to the circlet touching her forehead, Cassie felt a rush of tingling warmth. An—aliveness.

These are the real tools; not just symbols, she thought. They have power of their own.

In that moment, she knew she could direct their power. It was part of her, suffusing her with strength. She was a witch, from a line of powerful witches, and she was leader of this Circle.

"All right," she said, stepping out of the ring of stones and going over to take her Book of Shadows from her backpack. She was no longer worried about how she looked; she knew she looked good. That didn't matter. They had a little time ahead of them, and she wanted to use it to their advantage.

"All right, look; while we're waiting I think we should go through our Books of Shadows— my grandmother told me to study mine, and it's better than doing nothing," she said. "We can take turns reading out loud until it gets dark— he won't move until then."

"Are you sure?" Melanie said.

"Yes." Cassie didn't know how she knew, but she knew. Her grandmother had called it the Sight, but to Cassie it was more like a voice—

an inner voice, a voice at her core. By now, she knew enough to listen to it.

Nobody argued. Those who had them reached for Books of Shadows. Outside, the wind wailed dismally.

FIFTEEN

Around four o'clock the power went off. The house got colder. They lit candles and went on reading.

"'For Protection Against Fire and Water,'" Cassie read. But Melanie said the spell which came after wasn't powerful enough to protect against a hurricane, and Cassie knew she was right.

"Here, this is 'To Cast Out Fear and Malignant Emotions,'" Diana read from her own book. "'Sun by day/ and moon by night/ let all dark thoughts/ be put to flight.' Nice thought."

They went on reading. *A Charm to Cure a Sickly Child. An Amulet for Power. Three Spells to Bind a Lover. To Raise a Storm*—that, they didn't need, Cassie thought wryly. She read again about crystals: how the larger a crystal was, the more energy it could store and focus. The spell *To Turn Aside Evil*, she read aloud, although she didn't understand it.

"'Invoke the power which is yours alone, calling upon the elements or those features of the natural world which lie closest to your heart. These powers have you over all that is evil: powers of sun and moon and stars, and of everything belonging to the earth.'"

She read it again, puzzling. "I still don't get it."

"I think it means that as witches we can call on nature, on the things that are *good*, to fight evil," Melanie said.

"Yes, but how do we call on them?" Cassie said. "And what do they do when we do it?"

Melanie didn't know.

It got dark. The gray light from the windows got dimmer and dimmer and finally faded altogether. Wind banged the shutters and rattled the glass in the windows. The rain kept coming steadily in the blackness.

"What do you think he'll do?" asked Suzan.

"Something unfriendly," said Laurel.

Cassie was proud of them. They were scared;

she knew them well enough to know that fear was what was behind Deborah's restless pacing and Melanie's stillness, but none of them were running away or backing down. Doug cracked bad jokes, and Chris made paper airplanes. Nick sat tense and silent, and Adam kept Doug's headphones on, listening to the news on the radio.

At six o'clock the storm stopped.

Cassie's ears, used to the drumming of rain and the clattering and banging and howling of wind, felt suddenly empty. She looked and saw the others were all sitting alert.

"It can't be over," Suzan said. "Unless it missed us?"

"It's still out in the Atlantic," Adam said. "They think it should hit land in about an hour. This is just the calm before the storm."

"Cassie?" said Diana.

"I think he's making his move," Cassie said, trying to sound calm. And then every muscle in her body tightened.

Cassandra.

It was his voice in her mind. She looked at the others and saw they'd heard it too.

Bring your coven to the end of Crowhaven Road. To Number Thirteen, Cassandra. I'm waiting for you.

Cassie's fingers clenched on a piece of unfolded laundry lying nearby. She tried to concentrate on the power of the Master Tools, on the warmth where they touched her. Then she pushed with her mind, forming words.

We're coming. Say hello to Faye.

She let out her breath. Doug grinned at her. "Pretty good," he said.

It was sheer bravado, and they all knew it, but it made Cassie feel better. She inconspicuously wiped her wet palms on the laundry and stood up. "Let's go," she said.

Diana had been right; wearing the symbols of the coven leader and the white shift, she didn't feel cold. Outside, the sky was clear and the earth was silent except for the sound of the waves. Yes, the calm before the storm, Cassie thought. It was a very uneasy calm, ready to erupt into violence again at any moment.

Melanie said, "Look at the moon."

Cassie's stomach lurched.

It looked like a crescent moon, a silver disk with a bite out of it. But Cassie sensed the wrongness there. It wasn't a crescent moon; it was a full moon being invaded, overshadowed. She was watching darkness fall on a bright world.

She thought she could actually see the shadow moving, covering more of the white surface.

"Come on," she said.

They walked up the wet street, making for the headland. They passed Suzan's house with its Grecian pillars, a gray bulk against the moonlight. They passed Sean's house, just as dark. Water gurgled down the sides of the road in little rivers. They passed Cassie's house.

They reached the vacant lot at Number Thirteen.

It looked just the way it had when they had celebrated Halloween here by making a bonfire and calling up Black John's spirit. Empty, deserted. Barren. There was nobody here.

"Is it a trick?" Nick asked sharply. Cassie shook her head uncertainly. The little voice inside wasn't telling her anything. She looked eastward at the moon, and felt another shock.

It was visibly smaller, the crescent very thin now. The shadow was not black or gray, but a dull copper-brown color.

"Ten minutes until totality," Melanie said.

"About half an hour until the hurricane reaches land," said Adam.

A fresh wind blew around them. Cassie's feet,

in the thin white shoes Diana had brought for her, were damp.

They stood uncertainly. Cassie listened to the waves crashing at the base of the cliff. Her senses were alert, searching, but nothing seemed to be happening. Minutes dragged by and her nerves stretched more and more taut.

"Look," Diana whispered.

Cassie looked at the moon again.

The dull brownish shadow was swallowing up the last fingernail-thin edge of brightness. Cassie watched it go, like a candle winking out. Then she gasped.

The sound was involuntary and she was ashamed of it, but everyone else was gasping too. Because the moon hadn't just gone dark, like a new moon, and it wasn't even the coppery-brown color. As it was covered by shadow it turned red, a deep and ominous red, like old blood. High in the sky, perfectly visible, it glowed like a coal with unnatural light.

Then someone choked and Sean made a squealing noise.

Cassie turned quickly, in time to see it happening. On the empty lot before them, something was appearing. A rectangular bulk was taking shape, and as Cassie watched, it became more and more solid. She could see a steeply pitched roof, flat clapboard walls, small windows irregularly placed. A door made of heavy planks. It looked like the old wing of her grandmother's house, the original dwelling from 1693.

It shone with a dull light, like the blood-red moon.

"Is it real?" Deborah whispered.

Cassie had to wait a moment to get the breath to speak. "It's real *now*," she said. "Right now, for a few minutes, it's real."

"It's *horrible*," Laurel whispered.

Cassie knew what she was feeling, what the whole coven was feeling. The house was evil, in the same way that the skull was evil. It looked twisted, askew, like something out of a nightmare. And it gripped all of them with an instinctual terror. Cassie could hear Chris and Doug breathing hard.

"Don't go near it," Nick said tightly. "Everybody stay back until he comes out."

"Don't worry," Deborah assured him. "Nobody's going near that."

Cassie knew better.

The inner voice, silent just a few moments

ago, was telling her clearly now what she had to do. What it wasn't telling her was how to get up the courage to do it.

She looked behind her, at the rest of them standing there. The Club. The Circle. Her friends.

Ever since her initiation, Cassie had been so happy to be a part of this group. She'd relied on different members of it at different times, crying on Diana and clinging to Nick and Adam when she needed them. But now there was something she had to do, and not even Nick or Adam could help her with it. Not even Diana could go with her.

"I have to go alone," she said.

She figured out that she'd said it aloud when she saw them all staring at her. The next instant they were all protesting.

"Don't be crazy, Cassie. That's his territory; you can't go in there," Deborah said.

"Anything could happen. Let him come out," Nick told her.

"It's too dangerous. We won't let you go by yourself," Adam said flatly.

Cassie looked at him reproachfully, because he was the one who'd said that being coven leader might not be good for *her*; and he was right, so he was the one who should understand now. Of course this was dangerous, but she had to do it. Black John—John Blake—Jack Brunswick, whatever you wanted to call him—had summoned her here, and he was waiting for her inside. And Cassie had to go.

"If you didn't want to listen to me you shouldn't have elected me leader," she said. "But I'm telling you now, that's what he wants. He isn't coming out. He wants me to go in."

"But you don't have to," Chris said, almost pleading.

Of them all, only Diana was silent. She stood, mouth trembling, tears hanging on her lashes. It was to her that Cassie spoke.

"Yes, I do," she said.

And Diana, who understood about being a leader, nodded.

Cassie turned away before she could see Diana cry. "You stay here," she said to all of them, "until I come out. I'll be all right; I've got the Master Tools, remember?"

Then she started walking toward the house.

The nails in the heavy timber door were set in a pattern of swirls and diamonds. They seemed to glow redder than the wood around them. Cassie touched the iron door-handle hesitantly, but it was cool and solid to her fingers. The door swung open before her and she went inside.

Everything here was slightly misty, like a red hologram, but it *felt* real enough. The kitchen was much like her grandmother's kitchen and it was empty. The parlor next door was the same. A flight of narrow, winding stairs rose from the back corner of the parlor.

Cassie climbed the steps, noting with a strange amusement the incongruity of the tin lantern hanging on the wall. It was giving off a cold, eerie red light, barely brighter than the house itself. The stairs were steep and her heart was pounding when she reached the top.

The first small bedroom was empty. So was the second. That left only the large room over the kitchen.

Cassie walked toward it without faltering. On the threshold she saw that the red glow in here was brighter, like the surface of the shadowed moon.

She went in.

He was inside, standing so tall that his head almost touched the uneven ceiling. He was giving off a light of pure evil. His face was triumphant and cruel, and inside, Cassie thought she could see the outlines of the skull.

Cassie stopped and looked at him.

"Father," she said, "I've come."

"With your coven," Black John said. "I'm proud of you." He extended a hand to her, which she ignored.

"You brought them here very nicely," he went on. "I'm glad they had the sense to acclaim you as leader."

"It's only temporary," Cassie said.

Black John smiled. His eyes were on the Master Tools. "You wear them well," he said.

Cassie felt a slow writhe of panic in her stomach. Everything was going according to his plan, she could see that. She was here, with the tools he'd wanted for so long, on his territory, in his house. And she was afraid of him.

"There's no need to be frightened, Cassandra," he said. "I don't want to hurt you. We don't need to quarrel. We have the same purpose: to unify the coven."

"We don't have the same purpose."

"You are my daughter."

"I'm no part of you!" Cassie cried. He was playing on her emotions, looking for her weaknesses. And every minute the hurricane was getting closer to land. Cassie sought desperately for a distraction, and she glimpsed something behind the tall man.

"Faye," she said. "I didn't see you there, standing in his shadow."

Faye stepped forward indignantly. She was wearing the black silk shift, like a negative image of Cassie's, and her own diadem, bracelet, and garter. She lifted her head proudly and gazed at Cassie with smoldering golden eyes.

"My two queens," Black John said fondly. "Dark and bright. Together, you will rule the coven—"

"And you'll rule us?" Cassie asked sharply.

Black John smiled again. "It's a wise woman who knows when to be ruled by a man."

Faye wasn't smiling. Cassie looked at her sideways.

Black John didn't appear to notice. "Do you want me to stop the hurricane?" he asked Cassie.

"Yes. Of course." This was what she'd come for, to hear his terms. And to try and find his weak point. Cassie waited.

"Then all you have to do is swear an oath. A blood oath, Cassandra; you're familiar with those." He held a hand out to Faye without looking at her. Faye stared at the hand for an instant, then reached down to pull a dagger out of her garter. The black-handled knife used for casting circles on the ground. Black John held it up, then he cut his own palm. Blood welled out sluggishly, dark red.

Like Adam, Cassie thought wildly, her heart accelerating. Like the oath Adam and I swore.

The tall man held the dagger toward Cassie. When she made no move to step forward and take it, he held it toward Faye. "Give it to her," he said.

Faye took the dagger and handed it to Cassie, handle first. Slowly, Cassie's fingers grasped it. Faye moved back to Black John's side.

"It's just a little blood, Cassandra. Swear obedience to me and I'll release the hurricane, let it turn harmlessly back out to sea. Then you and I can begin our reign together."

The dagger was actually trembling in Cassie's hand. There was no way to steady her pulse now. She knew what she was going to do, but she needed time to get her nerve up.

"How did you kill Jeffrey?" she said. "And why?"

The tall man looked momentarily taken aback, then he recovered. "By getting him to sit down for a moment; and to cause dissent between our kind and the outsiders," he said.

He smiled. "Besides, I didn't like his attention to my daughter. He wasn't one of us, Cassandra."

Cassie wished Portia could see her "Mr. Brunswick" now. "Why did you use Sean?" she asked.

"Because he was weak, and he already wore a stone that I could influence," he said. "Why all these questions? Don't you realize—"

He broke off then and moved lightning fast. While he was in the middle of speaking, Cassie had thrown the dagger at him. She'd never thrown a knife before, but some ancestor who'd worn the Master Tools must have, because the bracelet seemed to guide her right arm, and the dagger flashed end over end straight toward Black John's heart. But the tall man was simply too quick. He caught the dagger in midair—by the blade—and stood holding it, looking at Cassie.

"That was unworthy of you, Cassandra," he said. "And hardly any way to behave to your father. Now I'm angry with you."

He didn't sound angry; his voice was cold as death and poisonous. Cassie had thought she'd been afraid before, but that had been nothing. Now she was truly afraid. Her knees were weak and the pounding of her heart shook her whole body.

Black John tossed the dagger back and it stuck in the floor in front of Cassie, quivering. "The hurricane is about to reach land," he said. "You don't have a choice; you've never had a choice. Take the oath, Cassandra. *Do it!*"

I'm frightened, Cassie thought. Please, I'm so frightened . . . She was wearing the Master Tools, but she had no idea how to use them.

"I am your father. Do as I tell you."

If only I knew how to use them . . .

"You have no power to defy me!"

"Yes, I do," Cassie whispered. In her mind, a door opened, a silver light dawned. Like the moon coming out of a shadow, it illuminated everything. She understood the spell to turn aside evil now. *Invoke the power which is yours alone . . . these powers have you over all that is evil . . .*

Suddenly, she felt as if a long line of witches were standing behind her. She was only the last, only one of them, and all their knowledge was hers. Their knowledge and their power. Words rose to her lips.

"Power of moon have I over thee," she said shakily.

Black John stared at her, seeming to recoil.

"Power of moon have I over thee," Cassie repeated, more strongly. "Power of sun have I over thee."

Black John stepped back.

Cassie stepped forward, searching for the next words in her mind. But she didn't say them. A voice said them for her, a voice behind her.

"Power of stars have I over thee. Power of planets have I over thee."

It was Diana, her fair hair stirred as if in a light wind. She came to stand behind Cassie, tall and proud and slender, like a silver sword. Cassie's heart swelled; she had never been more glad to have anybody disregard her instructions in her life.

"Power of tides have I over thee. Power of rain have I over thee," said Adam. He was right beside Diana, his hair shining like firelight, like rubies, in the red glow.

Deborah was behind him, her dark hair tumbling around a small face fierce with concentration. "Power of wind have I over thee," she said.

Nick joined her, his eyes cold and angry. "Power of ice have I over thee."

And Laurel. "Power of leaf have I over thee.

Power of root have I over thee."

And Melanie. "Power of rock have I over thee."

They were all here, all joining Cassie, adding their voices to hers. And Black John was cowering before them.

"Power of thunder have I over thee," Doug told him, and, "Power of lightning have I over thee," shouted Chris.

"Power of dew have I over thee," Suzan said, and pushed a small figure in front of her. It was Sean, and he was shaking, seemingly terrified to come face to face with the man who had controlled his mind. But his voice rose in a shriek.

"Power of blood have I over thee!"

Black John was against the red wall of the house now, and he looked shrunken. His features had lost definition, and the red glow had died, leaving him black in reality.

But there were only eleven in Cassie's coven; the Circle wasn't complete. And only a full Circle could stand against this man.

As Sean's yell died, Black John straightened. He took a step toward them, and Cassie's breath caught.

"Power of fire have I over thee!" a husky

voice cried, and he fell back. In astonishment, Cassie looked at Faye. The tall girl seemed to have gained height as Black John had lost it, and she looked every inch a barbarian queen as she stood glaring at him. Then she moved to stand beside Cassie. "Power of darkness have I over thee," she said, each word a stabbing knife. "Power of night have I over thee!"

Now, thought Cassie. He was weak, wounded, and they were united. Now, if ever, was the time to defeat him.

But neither Fire nor Water had done it before. Black John had been defeated twice, had died twice, but always he'd come back. If they were going to get rid of him permanently they had to do more than destroy his body. They had to destroy the source of his power—the crystal skull.

If we only had a larger crystal, Cassie thought. But there was no larger crystal. She thought desperately of the protruding outcrops of granite in New Salem . . . but they weren't crystal, they wouldn't hold and focus energy. Besides, she didn't just need a big crystal, she needed an *enormous* one. One so huge—so huge . . .

I like to think of crystals as a beach, she heard Melanie's laughing voice say in her mind. A *crystal is just fossilized water and sand . . .*

Along with the words came a picture. A glimpse of Cassie's own hand that first day on the beach at Cape Cod. "Look down," Portia had hissed, seeing Adam coming, and so Cassie had looked down, ashamed, staring at her own fingers trailing in the sand. In the sand that glittered with tiny flecks of garnet, with green and gold and brown and black crystals. A beach. A beach.

"With me!" Cassie shouted. "All of you think with me—give me your power! *Now!*"

She pictured it clearly, the long beach stretching parallel to Crowhaven Road. More than a mile of it, of crystal piled on crystal. She sent her thoughts racing toward it, gathering the power of the coven behind her. She focused on it, through it, looking now at Black John—at the crystal skull with its grinning teeth and its hollow eyes. And then she *pushed* with her mind.

She felt it go out of her, like a rush of heat, like a solar flare with the energy of the entire Circle driving it. It poured through her into the beach, and from the beach into Black John, focused and intensified, with all the power of Earth and Water combined. And this time when the skull exploded it was in a shattering rain of crystal like the blasted amethyst pendant.

There was a scream that Cassie would never forget. Then the floor of the house at Number Thirteen disappeared from under her feet.

SIXTEEN

"Are you okay?" Cassie asked Suzan, whom she happened to be lying on. "Is everybody okay?"

The Circle was lying scattered over the vacant lot as if some giant hand had dropped them. But everyone was moving.

"I think my arm's broken," Deborah said, rather calmly. Laurel crawled over to her to look at it.

Cassie stared around the lot. The house was gone. Number Thirteen was a barren piece of land again. And the light was changing.

"Look," Melanie said, her face turned up. This time there was joy and reverence in her voice.

The moon was showing silver again, just a thin crescent, but now the crescent was growing. The blood color was gone.

"We did it," Doug said, his blond hair disheveled more wildly than Cassie had ever seen it. He grinned. "Hey! We did it!"

"*Cassie* did it," Nick said.

"Is he really gone?" Suzan asked sharply. "Gone for good this time?"

Cassie looked around again, sensing nothing but brisk air and the endlessly moving sea. The earth was quiet. There was no light but moon and stars.

"I think he is," she whispered. "I think we won." Then she turned quickly to Adam. "What about the hurricane?"

He was fumbling at his belt with the radio. "I hope it's not broken," he said, and put the headphones on, listening.

Limping and crawling, they all gathered around him, and waited.

He kept listening, shaking his head, flicking the channels. His face was tense. Cassie saw Diana beside her, and reached out to take her hand. They sat together, hanging on. Then Adam sat straight suddenly.

"Gale force winds on Cape Cod . . . storm

moving northeast . . . northeast! It's turned! It's heading out to sea!"

The Henderson brothers cheered, but Melanie hushed them. Adam was talking again.

"High tides . . . flooding . . . but it's okay, nobody's hurt. Property damage, that's all. We did it! We really did it!"

"Cassie did it—" Nick was beginning again, irritably, but Adam had leaped up and grabbed Cassie and was whirling her in the air. Cassie shrieked and kept shrieking as he swooped her around. She hadn't seen Adam this happy since . . . well, she couldn't remember *when* she'd seen Adam this happy. Since the beach on Cape Cod, she guessed, when he'd flashed that daredevil smile at her. She'd forgotten, in their months of trouble, that grimness wasn't Adam's natural state.

Like Herne, she thought, when she was deposited, breathless and flushed, back on her feet. The horned god of the forest was a god of joyful celebration. Chris and Doug were trying to dance with her now, both together. Adam was waltzing Diana. Cassie collapsed, laughing, just as something large and furry hit her and rolled her over.

"Raj!" Adam said. "I told you to stay at home!"

"He's about as obedient as all of you," Cassie gasped, hugging the German shepherd as his wet tongue lapped her face. "But I'm glad you came. All you guys, not the dog," she said, looking around at them.

"We couldn't just *leave* you in there," Sean said.

Doug snickered, but he slapped the smaller boy on the back. "'Course not, tiger," he said, and rolled his eyes at Cassie.

Cassie was looking at Faye, who had been sitting a little apart from everyone else, the way Nick used to do. "I'm glad you came to join us too," she said.

Faye didn't look anything at all like a stenographer. Her mane of pitch-black hair was loose over her shoulders, and the black shift exposed more pale honey-colored skin than it covered. She looked a little bit like a panther and a lot like a jungle queen.

Her heavy-lidded golden eyes met Cassie's directly, and a small smile tugged at the corners of her lips.

Then she looked down. "I can do my nails red again, anyway," she said lazily.

Cassie turned away, hiding a smile of her own. That was probably as much acknowledgement

298

from Faye as she was ever going to get.

"If you guys are all finished yelling and dancing," Laurel said, in a carefully patient voice, "can we go home now? Because Deborah's arm *is* broken."

Cassie jumped up guiltily. "Why didn't you *say* so?"

"Aw, it's nothing," Deborah said. But she let Nick and Laurel help her up.

As they walked back, Cassie was struck by another thought. Her mother. Black John was dead, the hurricane was detoured, but what about her mother?

"Can we take Deborah to the crones?" she asked Diana.

"That's the best place, anyway," Diana said. "They know the most about healing." She looked at Cassie with understanding in her green eyes, then she took Cassie's hand and squeezed it.

I've got to prepare myself, Cassie thought as they approached Number Four. I've got to be ready. She could be dead. She could be just the same as when I left there . . . lying on that bed. She could stay that way forever.

Whatever happens, I kept my promise. I stopped Black John. He won't ever hurt her again.

Cassie glanced up at the moon before stepping up to Melanie's house. It was a thick crescent now, a fat happy moon. She took it as a good omen.

Inside, candles flickered. Cassie wondered for one wild instant if the three old ladies were still dancing around sky-clad, and then she saw the parlor. Great-aunt Constance was sitting as stiff as a ramrod on the rounded seat of a chair, immaculately dressed and looking very proper as she served tea by candlelight to her three guests.

To her *three* guests . . .

"*Mom!*" cried Cassie, and she ran forward, knocking over one of Great-aunt Constance's fragile chairs as she went. The next minute she was holding her mother, hugging her wildly on Aunt Constance's couch. And her mother was hugging back.

"Good heavens, Cassie," her mother said a few minutes later, pulling away slightly to look at her. "The way you're dressed . . ."

Cassie felt for the diadem, which had fallen askew. She settled it on her head and looked into her mother's eyes. She was so happy to see those eyes looking back at her, and seeing, that she forgot to answer.

Deborah's voice came from the hallway, tired

but proud. "She's our leader," she said. Then: "Anybody got an aspirin?"

"Well, obviously it isn't just temporary," Laurel said, looking nettled. "I mean, we *elected* you."

"And you came through," Deborah said, taking a large bite out of an apple with the hand that wasn't in a cast.

It was the next day. There was no school, because of minor storm damage and the disappearance of the principal. The Circle was enjoying the unseasonably mild weather by having a picnic in Diana's backyard.

"But we've got *two* leaders now," said Chris. "Or is Faye unelected?"

"Hardly," Faye said, with a withering glance.

Melanie shifted thoughtfully, her gray eyes considering. "Well, other covens have had more than one leader. The original coven did; remember, Black John was only *one* of the leaders. You could share with Faye, Cassie."

Cassie shook her head. "Not without Diana."

"Huh?" said Doug.

Nick directed an amused glance at her. "Diana might not want the honor," he said.

"I don't care," Cassie said, before Diana could

say anything. "I won't be leader without Diana. I'll quit. I'll go back to California."

"Look, you can't *all* be leaders," Deborah began.

"Why not?" Melanie asked, sitting up. "Actually, it's a good idea. You could be a triumvirate. You know, like in Roman times; they had three rulers."

"Diana might not want to," Nick repeated, with rising inflection. But Cassie got up and went over to her anxiously.

"You will, won't you?" she said. "For me?"

Diana looked at her, then at the rest of the Club.

"Yeah, go on," Doug said expansively.

"Three's a good number," Laurel added, smiling impishly.

Faye sighed heavily. "Oh, why not?" she grumbled, looking in the other direction.

Diana looked at Cassie. "All right," she said.

Cassie hugged her.

Diana pushed a strand of fair hair back. "Now I've got something for you to do," she said. "As a leader, you're not a junior member of the coven anymore, Cassie, but nobody else can do this. Will you please go and dig up that box I gave you on the night of Hecate?"

302

"The trust festival box? Is this the time to unbury it?"

"Yes," Diana said. "It is." She was looking at Melanie and Melanie was nodding at her, obviously sharing some secret.

Cassie looked at both of them, puzzled, but then she went down the road to get the box, accompanied only by Raj, who trotted along behind her. It was wonderful to be alone, and to know that nothing was out to get her. She dug in the sand near the big rock where she'd buried it that night, and pulled the damp box out. The sea flashed and sparkled at her.

She brought it back to Diana's house, breathless from the walk, and presented it to Diana.

"What's in there? More Master Tools?" Doug said.

"It's probably some girl thing," said Chris.

Diana bent over the box, an odd expression on her face. "You didn't open it," she said to Cassie.

Cassie shook her head.

"Well, I know you didn't," Diana said. "I knew you wouldn't. But I wanted *you* to know. Anyway, it's yours; and what's inside it, too. It's a present." She blew drying sand off the box and handed it back to Cassie.

303

Cassie looked at her doubtfully, then shook the box. It rattled lightly, as if there were something small inside. She glanced at Diana again. Then, hesitantly, with an almost scared feeling, she opened it.

Inside, there was only one object. A little oval of rock, pale blue swirled with gray, embedded all over with tiny crystals which sparkled in the sunlight.

The chalcedony rose.

Every muscle frozen but her eyes, Cassie looked at Diana. She didn't know what to do or say. She didn't understand. But her heart was beating violently.

"It's yours," Diana said again, and then, as Cassie just crouched there, immobile, she looked at Melanie. "Maybe you'd better explain."

Melanie cleared her throat. "Well," she said, and looked over at Adam, who was sitting as still as Cassie. He hadn't said much all morning, and now he was staring at Diana wordlessly, riveted.

"Well," Melanie said again. Adam still wouldn't look at her, so she went on anyway. "It was when Adam was telling us about how he met you," she said to Cassie. "He described a connection—what you called a silver cord. You remember that?"

"Yes," said Cassie, not moving otherwise. She was looking at Diana now too, searching Diana's face. Diana looked back serenely.

"Well, the silver cord is something real, something in the old legends. The people it connects are soul mates—you know, meant to be together. So when Diana and I heard about it, we knew that's what you and Adam are," Melanie finished, sounding glad to be done explaining to people who wouldn't look at her.

"That was why I was surprised about Nick, you see," Diana said to Cassie, gently. "Because I knew you could only love Adam. And I was going to tell you at the very beginning, but then you were asking me to give you another chance, to let you prove you could be faithful . . . and I thought that was a good idea. Not for me, but for you. So you'd know, Cassie, how strong you are. Do you see?"

Cassie nodded mutely. "But—Diana—" she whispered.

Diana blinked, her emerald eyes misting over. "Now you're going to make me cry," she said. "Cassie, with all the unselfishness that's been going on around here, do you think I'm not going to do my part? You two have been waiting for months because of me. Now you don't have to wait anymore."

"There's nothing anybody can do about it," Melanie put in, sympathetically but pragmatically. "You and Adam are linked, and that's it. There isn't anyone else for either of you, so you're stuck together for this lifetime. Maybe for a lot of lifetimes."

Cassie, still frozen, shifted her eyes to Adam.

He was looking at Diana. "Diana, I can't just . . . I mean, I'll always—"

"I'll always love you, too," Diana said steadily. "You'll always be special to me, Adam. But it's Cassie you're in love with."

"Yes," Adam whispered.

Cassie looked down at the rough little stone in her palm. It was sparkling crazily and she felt very dizzy.

"Go on, go over to him," Diana said, pushing her gently.

But Cassie couldn't, so he came to her. He looked a bit dazed, but his eyes were as blue as the ocean in sunlight, and the way he smiled at her made her blush.

"Go on, kiss her," Chris said. Laurel smacked him. The rest of the Circle looked on with great interest.

Adam glared at them and kissed Cassie

formally on the cheek. Then, under cover of the groans, he whispered "Later," to her in a way that made her pleasantly nervous.

Can I handle Herne? she wondered, looking up at his hair that was so many colors: dark like garnet and bright like holly berries, threaded with gold in the sunshine. I guess I'm going to have to, she thought. For a lifetime, Melanie had said; maybe a lot of lifetimes.

For some reason that made her look at Faye and Diana.

She didn't know why, and then she had a flash of memory. Sunlight. Golden sunlight, the smell of jasmine and lavender, a laughing voice singing. Kate. Kate's hair had been the impossible fair color of Diana's. But, Cassie realized now, Kate's laughing, teasing eyes had been *Faye's*.

An ancestress of both of them, Cassie thought. After all, they're cousins; they've got most of their ancestors in common.

But something deep inside her seemed to smile, and she wondered. Was Melanie right; was it possible to have more than one life? Could a soul keep coming back to Earth? And if so, could a soul ever—split?

"I think," she said suddenly to Diana, "that

you and Faye are going to have to learn to get along. I think you two . . . need each other."

"Of course," Diana said, as if it were something everybody knew. "But why?"

It was probably a crazy theory. Cassie wouldn't tell her about it, or at least not right now. Maybe tomorrow.

"I'm going to do a picture, I believe," Diana was saying thoughtfully, "to add to my collection. What do you think of the Muse, with the moon and stars around her, looking inspired?"

"I think it's a good idea," Cassie said unsteadily.

"What we really have to talk about," said Melanie, "is what we're going to do with the Master Tools now. We have power; the coven has power, and we need to decide what to do with it."

"Naw, what we need to do is *party*," Doug said. "To make up for all the birthdays that we missed. Chris and me didn't get a real party, and neither did Sean or Laurel . . ."

"Environmentalism," Laurel was saying firmly to Melanie. "That should be our first cause."

"I didn't get a party either," Suzan pointed out, delicately peeling the wrapper off a Twinkie.

Faye examined her nails, jewel-red, in the sunlight. "I know some people I want to hex," she said.

Cassie looked at them all, her coven, laughing and arguing and debating with each other. She looked at Nick, who was leaning back, looking amused, and he caught her eye and winked.

Then she looked at Diana, whose clear green eyes shone at her for a moment. Then, "Yes, environmentalism is good," Diana said, turning to Laurel. "But we have to think about how to improve relations with the outsiders, too . . ."

Cassie looked at Adam and found him looking at her. He took her hand, closing it in his own, both of them holding the chalcedony rose.

Cassie looked down at their intertwined fingers, and it seemed that she could see the silver cord again, wrapping around their two hands, connecting them. But not just them. Filaments of the cord seemed to web out and touch the others of the group, linking them together with silver light. They were all connected, all part of one another, and the light shone around them to touch the earth and sky and sea.

Sky and sea, keep harm from me. Earth and fire, bring my desire.

They had. And they would in the future. With her inner vision, Cassie saw that the Circle was part of something bigger, like a spiral that went on and on forever, encompassing everything, touching the stars.

"I love you," Adam whispered.

From the center of the Circle, Cassie smiled.